BLUEBEARD'S CURSE

Dark Tales

REGINE ABEL

COVER DESIGN BY
Regine Abel

ILLUSTRATIONS BY
Astor Alexander
Vvevelur

CONTENTS

BLUEBEARD'S CURSE

Can you resist temptation?

King Erik Thorsen, also known as Bluebeard, is once more widowed. Like all the others before her, his late wife succumbed to the lure of the curse that plagues him and threatens the realm.

As willing maidens gather at the castle in the hope of being chosen, Erik sets his sights on a golden beauty named Astrid. However, becoming his queen comes with a steep price. The King's new bride must first resist temptation for one year and one day... or die trying.

Will Astrid be next to fall to what lies beyond the Sealed Door?

DEDICATION

To my family, who has always been there for me, believed in me, and had my back through every hurdle thrown my way.

To anyone who believes that love truly conquers all.

CHAPTER 1
ERIK

Hidden in the shadows of the balcony overlooking the ballroom, I observed the sea of maidens gathering in my home. Before the night's end, I would claim one of them as my twenty-eighth bride. How long she would last was anyone's guess. Six months had been the longest; twenty-four hours the shortest. And yet, despite these grim odds, still they vied to become my queen.

Their voices rose, a buzzing swarm of insects over the light music played by the orchestra. Hilda Lund's occasional boisterous laughter broke the monotony of the irritating hum. If only I could kick them all out. I approached the location where Hilda was holding court, amidst the other daughters of Rathlin's nobility.

They gaped at her, their faces flushed with excitement. Then again, the vermillion of their cheeks could be the result of the powder caked upon them or the ridiculous tightness of their bodices. As I discreetly leaned over the railing to eavesdrop on their conversation, the smell of their mixed perfumes overwhelmed me.

"It was a sign that my poor betrothed met with an untimely

demise less than a week ago," Hilda said to her captive audience. "I always believed that I was meant to free our beloved King Erik from the curse that plagues him and our people."

I almost snorted at her arrogance. She genuinely seemed convinced that she was the answer to all my woes; that somehow, she was a divine gift bestowed upon mankind. Hilda was a pretty thing in her royal purple dress. As lovely and venomous as a bouquet of wolfsbane. Maybe I should take her as wife and rid us all of her insufferable presence, once she failed like all the others.

"But all his previous wives have died. How will any of us make it? What is the test that's so impossible to pass?" a frail-looking redhead asked.

"They were weak," Hilda said with a shrug. "I'm not."

Yes. Weak, greedy, and self-centered. Most had also been arrogant... like her.

"Ariana lasted a little over six months," a brunette said in a conspiratorial tone. "Everyone thought she would complete the year, and yet she failed, too."

"Ariana was a dreamer. If not for the terrible illness that struck me last summer, I would have attended that gathering. King Erik would have chosen me instead," Hilda said. "I could have spared him this useless anguish."

This was more than I could bear. I stepped away from the balcony's railing, refusing to acknowledge the pain settling in my chest. Ariana had indeed been a dreamer, a sweet little thing who I too believed would have made it. I hadn't loved her, but I had grown to care for her. When we had passed the fifth month mark with her resolve still strong, I had thought this time, this wife wouldn't let me down. And yet...

My eyes scanned the room, assessing the three dozen maidens gathered within. The largest group surrounded Hilda, no doubt hoping to become part of her retinue, should I choose her. Others were scattered in smaller groups of twos and threes. But it was a lone figure by the large bay window that caught my attention.

Golden maiden...

She was tall and deliciously curvy in her long white dress. Blonde hair streaked with gold cascaded in waves down to her waist. Two beaded-braids framed a reasonably attractive pixie face. Biting nervously on her plump bottom lip, she observed the women mingling around the room. As if sensing my stare, she looked towards the balcony, her gaze landing directly where I stood. It sent an electric jolt down my spine and set my blood on fire. I instinctively took a step back, even though I knew she couldn't see me. She frowned while her stunning amber eyes examined the length of the balcony, before resuming her casual observation of the other women.

What the hell just happened?

No woman had ever stirred such a strong response from me —it intrigued me.

I gestured to Tormund, who had been shadowing me. When he approached, I pointed at the golden maiden with my chin.

"Her name is Astrid Halvar, your Highness," Tormund whispered. "She was promised to Lord Dennar's second son, but he reneged on his pledge once her family fell on hard times. Though her reputation is flawless, her prospects remain limited. The people would approve this choice."

"And you, Tormund?" I asked.

"She was well-loved by their servants, when they could still afford them. This would save her family from becoming destitute."

Typical Tormund answer. My majordomo always looked at problems in a practical way. He assessed each aspiring bride in terms of her potential longevity and for the benefits to those she would leave behind.

I nodded before making my way down to the dance floor. The guards opened the large double doors, causing silence to submerge the room. The maidens rushed to line up in a cacophony of scraping chairs, and the clinking of glasses quickly discarded on nearby tables. Hilda elbowed her way to the middle of the lineup. She gave me a toothy smile, pushing her corseted bosom towards me.

My gaze glided over her and the other maidens until it settled on Astrid. Her eyes widened as I started walking in her direction. Astrid's lips parted in astonishment, and she cast an uncertain glance at the others before looking back at me. She swallowed audibly when I stopped in front of her.

"Welcome to my home, Lady Astrid. Would you do me the honor of the first dance?" I asked, extending my hand.

"It would be my pleasure, your Highness." Despite her steady voice, the hand she placed in mine trembled.

I led her to the center of the dance floor under Hilda's outraged glare. Astrid's delicate hand slid over my shoulder as I wrapped my arm around her waist, pulling her tightly against me. A soft gasp erupted from her slender throat, but she didn't challenge our proximity. I nodded to the conductor. The notes of a waltz reverberated in the large, circular room. Astrid followed my lead effortlessly as we whirled across the floor under the stares of the other maidens.

She looked beautiful up close. A handful of freckles peppered her dainty little nose. Her flawless skin, the color of honey, looked good enough to lick. I wished she didn't keep her eyes demurely cast down, wondering how much fire hid behind them. Halfway through the song, Astrid's hand tensed in mine when I pulled her even closer. It was inappropriate, but I didn't care—I loved the way her luscious body aligned perfectly with mine. Her voluptuous chest rose rapidly with each breath. She was soft and pliant in my arms. I leaned forward, inhaling the delicate scent of lavender that emanated from her. She licked her lips nervously, and I fought the sudden urge to taste them.

"Tell me, Lady Astrid, did you come to the lair of Bluebeard of your own free will, or did your family coerce you into it?"

Her eyes locked onto my beard and its three beaded braids, before lifting back up to mine. "My father didn't want me to come, your Highness. He fears…"

"He fears you will fail like my previous brides," I finished for her when the silence stretched. She nodded, her eyes cast down. "Are you so confident then that you will prevail where all others have floundered?"

She tensed and pulled back from me. Her thin eyebrows, a shade darker than her hair, pinched in a frown. "No, your Highness. I wouldn't be so presumptuous. My family will be destitute unless I secure a good husband. So whatever the challenge, I will face it head-on for the sake of my father and little sister."

"Whatever the challenge? Even the monster of Rathlin?" I asked softly.

Astrid's gaze roamed over my face, taking in my features. "I see no monster."

"Eyes are easily deceived, milady. Twenty-seven maidens I have called wife over the past fourteen years. What manner of man goes through so many, each never to be heard from or seen again?"

A hint of fear crossed her face before she schooled her expression. Good. Naïve and simple-minded wouldn't survive what awaited her.

"A man cursed for saving Rathlin from the true monster that haunted its shores," she said. "Are you to blame because the maidens accepted a challenge they couldn't complete?"

I stopped dancing so abruptly she almost stumbled into me. With a surprised sound, Astrid tightened her hold on me to keep her balance.

"And what do you suppose the nature of this challenge is?"

She frowned, her eyes taking a faraway look as if pondering

my question. "I have wondered that many times, your Highness. But I must confess, I have no idea."

Leaning forward, I brushed my lips against her ear before whispering, "It's temptation, Lady Astrid. Can you resist temptation?"

Her breath caught in her throat. I pulled back to look into her eyes. She shivered, and goosebumps erupted all over her golden skin.

"Temptation comes in many forms, your Highness. I'm not covetous by nature. And as someone who treasures her privacy, I have little inclination to pry into other people's personal matters."

She had all the right answers. Whether they were genuine or rehearsed was anyone's guess. I loved the sultriness of her voice though and couldn't help wondering how she would sound shouting my name in the throes of passion. Images of her writhing beneath me, her amber eyes burning with desire, flooded my mind. My blood rushed to my groin.

"Good answer, milady. But not all temptations are bad."

Heat crept up her cheeks when I pressed my blossoming arousal against her. She licked her lips nervously again, her hands still gripping me fiercely.

"The maiden I choose will be my wife in every way, Lady Astrid. I'm a man with a healthy appetite. Can you face *that* challenge head on?"

She swallowed hard, and I felt her tremble in my arms. At that moment, I realized how badly I wanted her to say yes. Whatever answer I expected, it wasn't her pressing her chest against mine or the words she whispered.

"*That* will not be a challenge."

Her face went crimson with embarrassment, but she didn't avert her eyes. My cock was now fully stiff. Astrid's breathing became erratic. I leaned forward, intent on tasting her parted lips when the pungent scent of Hilda's perfume ruined the moment.

Turning my head, I saw her approaching with her usual too bright smile.

"If it pleases your Highness, I would like to claim the second dance," she said with false enthusiasm.

I had been so lost in Astrid, the music stopping never even registered. My displeasure at the unwelcome interruption must have shown on my face. Hilda seemed to lose some of her confidence and cast a nervous glance around the room. She suddenly realized the humiliation that would befall her should I... *when* I dismissed her.

Astrid tried to take a step away from me. I tightened my embrace, wanting her voluptuous body flush against mine, and against the stiffness that ached for her.

I looked back at the golden maiden. "Consider this unpleasant intrusion your one and only chance to run, Lady Astrid. Think carefully and choose wisely."

Her eyes widened in understanding. This wasn't the most romantic proposal, but this also was no traditional courtship. It baffled me that I offered her an out. By law, no maiden could refuse me. Though I didn't force any to present themselves whenever I needed a new bride, those who showed up—and many always did—implicitly gave their consent by entering the castle. Yet, for some reason, I wanted to hear this young beauty give herself to me freely.

"Why would I run when I'm exactly where I want to be?" Astrid asked.

Such boldness delighted me. I smiled.

"There will be no second dance," I said to Hilda, my eyes still locked with Astrid's.

"What?" Hilda exclaimed, shock and outrage filling her voice. "You have to! You can't—"

My head snapped towards her. "Do you presume to tell me what I can and cannot do, Madam?" I challenged, my voice deadly calm.

She shook her head as her throat worked. "O–of course not, y–your Highness."

Tormund approached in the deafening silence and extended his arm to Hilda. "This way, if you please, milady."

Her powdered face grew even paler. Hurt and disbelief flickered in her eyes. I almost felt sorry for her. Almost... Hilda put a shaky hand on Tormund's forearm, and he escorted her off the dance floor. He gestured to the other maidens to follow him before leading them out of the ballroom. I nodded at the conductor. The music soon drowned the clip-clopping of the maidens' receding footsteps as the orchestra launched into another waltz. Astrid smiled, her face filled with wonder as we twirled and whirled around the circular room.

What conscience I had left berated me for allowing my lust to condemn this delightful creature to die well before her time— by my own hand. And die she would, before the year was up. The strength of my attraction to her made little sense, yet it couldn't be denied; I had to have her. However, for the weeks— with luck, months—she had left, I vowed to make her happy. As for those she left behind, they would never want for anything, ever again.

Thus, I had chosen my new bride, Astrid Halvar—Bluebeard's twenty-eighth wife.

CHAPTER 2
ASTRID

In a complete daze, I abandoned myself to the strong arms of the fearsome Sea King of Rathlin Islands. The massive chandelier above us, and the two dozen torches and candelabras lining the walls, bathed the hall in a soft, dreamlike glow. As we glided across the floor, the light gave King Erik's raven hair and beard a midnight blue tinge. His silver-gray eyes hypnotized me. His large hand on my lower back held me firmly against his hard, muscular body.

Despite my lack of experience, I recognized the stiffness straining against my stomach for what it was. Though I was pretty enough, the obvious signs of his arousal had taken me by surprise. Ladies earned praises for their narrow waists and slender limbs. While my more luscious curves often attracted approving masculine gazes, I didn't understand how they had ensnared the King. Many of the most beautiful daughters of the realm had been in attendance tonight. Like the other maidens, I believed Hilda would be chosen.

When I defied my father's wishes by attending the gathering, I didn't think I stood a chance. My family's dire financial situation commanded me to act—even if only to say I didn't passively accept our fate. Fully aware of my humbled station, the other ladies had shunned me. It didn't bother me as I never cared to be popular or sought other people's approval. The King should have given me the same treatment though. So when he set his entire focus on me instead, all rational thoughts flew out of my head.

I couldn't believe how wantonly I had pressed my chest to his. He affected me in ways I never anticipated. There was such hunger in his eyes. His deep, raspy voice was mesmerizing, hypnotic even. When he made clear he expected full intimacy, the strangest heat blossomed in the pit of my stomach and radiated down my legs. It shamed me to admit I took pleasure in Hilda's humiliation when he sent her away, and not only because she always looked down on me. In truth, I had wanted to be King Erik's chosen.

But now that my wish had come true, I wasn't so certain anymore. The last notes of the waltz faded, and we stood still in the center of the dance floor. King Erik's hand left my lower back for barely a second, and then resumed its tight embrace. Muted shuffling and the scraping of chairs informed me the orchestra was making an exit. I realized Erik must have gestured for them to leave. I tried to swallow, but my throat was too dry. My heart hammering, I looked into the steely eyes that seemed to want to capture my soul.

"I've dismissed all the other maidens. Do you know what that means?" he asked softly.

My throat felt too tight to speak, but somehow I managed. "Y–Yes, your Highness."

"Erik," he corrected. "I would have my bride call me by my given name."

I couldn't help the violent shudder that coursed through me. His bride... Bluebeard's wife. What was I thinking, coming here? Over two dozen women, many made of sterner stuff than me, had miserably failed whatever challenge now awaited me. What arrogance had driven me to freely enter the dragon's lair, thinking I could walk back out unscathed? The triumphant elation I had felt when Tormund escorted the other maidens out was already a distant memory. In its stead, the pressing urge to race after them and return to the safety of my father's estate soared within me.

No doubt having sensed my rising panic, Erik's eyes narrowed. His lips lost the soft incline of his seductive smile as his expression hardened.

"It's too late to be having second thoughts, little girl. You had your chance to run. You're mine now."

"I–I'm not having second thoughts, your High... Erik." I hated that I was acting unusually squeamish. "My nerves are finally catching up to me, that's all. This is so... unexpected."

His expression told me he didn't believe me. However, he didn't press the issue. Instead, he released me from the intimate embrace he had held me in from the moment we launched into our first dance. The loss of his warm, strong body wrapped around mine left me feeling bereft rather than relieved. My reactions made no sense, even to me. At first, I wanted to run, but once he let go, I wanted to be held.

Erik took a step back and offered me his arm. Accepting the gallant gesture, I let him escort me out of the ballroom. The guards closed the door behind us, and we crossed the deserted hallway into the small chapel located a few doors down. It was a large rectangular room. A crimson carpet separated two rows of eight benches leading up to a stone altar. Behind it, Father Osvald stood by a ten-foot high, intricately carved Celtic cross.

My father had looked forward to giving me away on my wedding day. But here I stood in an empty chapel, bathed in the soft glow of moonlight streaking through the large, vaulted windows and the flickering of candelabras. The scent of burning candles mingled with the spicy aroma of incense. Tormund lingered by the altar, probably to bear witness. A long tri-color braided cord rested on the altar before Father Osvald.

Not a wedding... a handfasting...

Of course, that made sense. Why go through the expenses and logistical nightmare of a full ceremony if the new wife didn't last more than a handful of months? Not to mention the legal implications involved with rules of succession should he have married all his previous brides. The handfasting lasted one year and one day. It was a legally binding union during which the bride and groom could test their compatibility before committing to a permanent marriage. In my case, it would be to test my ability to resist whatever temptation I would be subjected to.

Father Osvald seemed stricken when he recognized me at Erik's side. There was no need to ask why. I did a lot of charity work whenever I could afford the time. Father Osvald and I had developed a respectful friendship over the years. Clearly, he believed I was doomed. He schooled his features before bowing to Erik. Well, to *us*...

He took the braided cord on the altar before circling around to stand before Erik and me. Our eyes met, and I gave him a nervous smile. He responded with a strained one.

"King Erik Thorsen, Lady Astrid Halvar, is it your wish that your hands be fasted this day?" Father Osvald solemnly asked.

"It is," Erik and I said in unison.

His voice was firm, deep and gravelly. Mine was breathy, but at least it didn't shake.

"As your hands are fasted, remember well that these cords are not the real ties that bind," Father Osvald said, holding the cords up.

Erik lifted his left hand, and I placed my right one on top of his. Father Osvald slowly began to wrap the braided cords around our hands.

"May you be forever bound as one, man and woman, with these cords as the symbol of your unity. A white cord, as a sign of purity, so you may begin with a clean slate. A purple cord, so your spiritual strength never falters in the face of adversity. A blue cord so that you may forever remain faithful to each other and steadfast in upholding all promises exchanged."

I was grateful for the strength of Erik's hand beneath mine. Reality was finally sinking in, and slivers of fear crept down my spine.

The wrapping completed, Father Osvald held our hands between his. "May you be forever as one in passion, devotion, and respect. King Erik, Lady Astrid, your hands are bound. You are now husband and wife. Your Highness, you may kiss your bride."

Turning to face me, Erik folded his bound arm towards his shoulder, pulling me to him in the process. His free hand wrapped around my neck, his thumb gently lifting my face to his. My lips parted while his descended to brush against mine. His mouth was soft and warm… at first. Erik's hand slipped to the back of my head, his fingers sneaking through my hair. The pressure of his lips intensified, then his tongue invaded my mouth. He tasted like spice and burnt caramel, as if he had recently enjoyed a glass of rum.

I wasn't much of a drinker, unable to handle alcohol too well, but Erik's kiss was going to my head faster than any liquor I'd ever had. My nipples hardened, while a dull throbbing between my legs seemed to pulsate in sync with my hammering heart. I couldn't contain the moan that escaped me. Erik's hand fisted in my hair in response, and the kiss intensified for a second before he tore himself away. I almost whimpered at the loss. The gray of his eyes was stormy with desire and shone with promises of the night to come. I shivered with anticipation.

Father Osvald removed the cords binding our hands then folded them neatly on the altar. He unrolled two parchments— the copies of the handfasting contract. After we both signed and Tormund witnessed, Erik apposed his royal seal on the copy that would be sent to my father along with my bride token.

For this alone, the challenge I would face over the next year was worth it. Whether I succeeded or failed no longer mattered, beyond the fact that I wasn't ready to die. While I didn't know the details of my bride token, it would be generous enough to ensure the financial welfare of my family.

After another respectful bow, Father Osvald left. Rather than following him to have the contract and bride token delivered to my father, Tormund approached us. He presented an ornate jeweled box to Erik, who opened it. Resting on a black velvet cushion was a magnificent golden necklace with a gem-encrusted medallion in the shape of a nautilus. At the center of the spiral, a large pearl glowed with a slow, steady pulse.

Erik took the necklace out of the box and fastened it around my neck. I was so fascinated by the pulsating gem that I barely noticed Tormund's quiet departure. My breath caught in my throat when the pendant came to rest between my breasts. It was as if a connection had been established between the gem and something within me. I cast a worried look at Erik, who stared at me intently.

"I–I felt something," I said, my voice uncertain. "Is that normal? It will not hurt me, will it?"

"Yes, it is normal. And no, it will not hurt you. Quite the opposite."

He caressed the medallion with the back of two fingers. The side of his hand brushed the inner curve of my breast. I barely repressed a shiver while goosebumps once again erupted all over my skin. A knowing smile blossomed on his lips, and my cheeks heated.

"You must never remove it, under any circumstances. Not to bathe, not to sleep, never… not until the end of our handfasting. Do you understand me?"

"Yes, Erik."

His intensity unnerved me.

"Swear it, Astrid."

His insistence gave me pause.

"Is this the challenge? To never remove it for a year?"

"No. While it does play a part in it, wearing the medallion isn't the challenge. That will begin tomorrow. I will tell you what you need to know about it then. For now, I want your word. Swear it, Astrid."

I didn't know where my sudden reluctance stemmed from. I knew, coming here, that I would be required to commit to something that would put my welfare at risk. I had accepted that eventuality, even though I hadn't expected to be chosen. Maybe it was the sense of finality that came with making such a pledge.

"I–I swear not to remove the necklace for any reason until the end of our handfasting."

Erik seemed... relieved. For a moment, I thought he was going to say something. Instead, he cupped my face in his hands and hungrily captured my mouth with his. My lips instinctively parted, and I clung to his shoulders like a drowning woman. Our tongues mingled for a while. His hands caressed my neck and slid down to my shoulders. Moaning softly, I pressed myself against him. I eagerly awaited the moment his strong hands would wrap around me and pull me close, as he had earlier on the dance floor. Instead, they pushed back on my shoulders as he ended our kiss, putting distance between us. I looked up at him in confusion.

"Such enthusiasm," Erik said with a seductive smile. "I want you, Astrid... but not in a chapel."

His words were like freezing rain on the embers of my arousal. I looked around the room in a haze. How could I have forgotten so quickly where we were? My face crimson with embarrassment, I followed Erik as he led me out.

The castle was massive... and scary. Our footsteps echoed in the eerie silence that surrounded us. The further we went into the castle, the more dark shadows seemed to encroach on the receding number of areas lit by torches or chandeliers.

"Where is everyone?" I whispered.

It was silly, but I felt as if speaking at a normal level would alert nightmarish creatures lurking in the darkness, and they would descend upon us.

Frowning, Erik stared at me for a moment. "The servants and the guards don't stay within the castle at night. They will return in the morning. Should you ever have need of them at night, there is a bell you can ring from our bedchamber."

That made me uneasy. "Why would everyone leave the castle?"

"Because it isn't safe for them," Erik said with a shrug.

That stopped me dead in my tracks, and I pulled away the hand that had been resting on his forearm. Erik turned to face me, his expression unreadable.

"Why is it unsafe for them?" I was proud of the steadiness of my voice despite my increasing worry. "Are they afraid of you? Is that why you called yourself a monster?"

He sighed and took a step towards me. On instinct, I backed away. His face immediately hardened. My anxiety level escalated at the sudden change.

"Don't do that," Erik said through gritted teeth. "Don't ever run away from me, Astrid."

The pitch of his voice had changed. It had been so subtle that, without a trained musical ear, I might have missed it. But it triggered the strangest reaction within me. My feet suddenly felt heavy, like rooted in place.

I glanced over my shoulder at the way back towards the entrance before staring warily at him. Right now, there was nothing I wanted more than to do exactly that; run as fast as my legs allowed. However, not only would he easily catch me, even had I not been wearing a long dress, I felt at a visceral level that I couldn't explain that my feet wouldn't obey me. Instead, I hugged my midsection to hide the trembling of my hands.

"You're scaring me, Erik."

He sighed. "There's no reason for you to be afraid of me,

Astrid. I'm the last person who wants to see you come to harm. You're the key to breaking the curse." He slowly closed the distance between us, and I fought the urge to back away again. "The threat that keeps the servants and the guards away from the castle isn't me."

"Then who?" I glanced at the shadows, forcing myself to remain calm. "Is there someone else here with us? Something else? What do they fear?"

Erik cupped my face between his hands. "Temptation."

CHAPTER 3
ERIK

I t took a while to alleviate some of Astrid's fears. She wasn't like my previous brides, and I didn't know if it was a good or a bad thing. With the others, it hadn't been until the second or third day, in some cases an entire week, before they realized that the castle slowly emptied with the setting of the sun. Such sensitivity and situational awareness could mean trouble in light of the year that lay ahead of her.

But right this instant, the curse was the last thing I wanted to dwell on. Astrid walked around the master bedroom, looking at everything but me, or the massive four poster bed next to the stone wall. I added another log to the fireplace, then turned back to her. I could see the apprehension on her face, mixed with a healthy dose of anticipation. In the next few minutes, it was passion and desire I wanted to put there.

I unfastened my belt before tossing it onto the chair in the sitting area facing the fireplace. Astrid stared at me wide-eyed and chewed her bottom lip with a row of pearly-white teeth. Her golden skin glowed under the flickering light of the fireplace. I pulled off my thigh-length tunic and threw it next to the belt. The rise and fall of her corseted breasts accelerated as I closed the distance between us. I stood in front of her, bare-chested. Astrid's amber eyes roamed over me, darkening with arousal. Her pink tongue peeking through her plump lips to moisten them sent a jolt of desire straight to my cock.

"Do you want to touch me, Astrid?" I asked in a soft voice.

Her face heated. She tucked her hair behind her ear, then nodded.

"I'm your husband. My body is yours to do with as you please. Touch me. I want to feel your hands on me."

She raised her hands hesitantly and let them hover near my chest, not making contact. I ached for her touch. Unable to wait any longer, I grabbed her hands and placed them on my chest. She made a startled sound but didn't resist.

"See? It's not that hard. Go on, my bride. Explore what's yours."

Her hands were soft and warm, wandering over my chest. It was the most exquisite torture. I could feel myself hardening, straining against my breeches. The desire to tear off her dress, toss her on the bed, and bury myself to the hilt inside her was nearly overwhelming. But my bride was a virgin. I needed her to get comfortable with me before I began peeling off her clothes. She circled my nipples with her fingers. Her touch was clumsy yet incredibly erotic. A deep moan rumbled out of my chest.

"You like that?" she asked, clearly seeking reassurance.

"Yes. Your hands feel amazing on my skin. Kiss me."

She giggled nervously but complied. Lifting her face to mine, she rose on the tips of her toes to reach my lips. Tilting my head down, I captured hers. Once she relaxed against me, I teased the seam of her mouth with my tongue until she granted me access. She tasted sweet like honeyed wine. I took my time, exploring, savoring. Though timid at first, her tongue began to respond eagerly to mine.

Astrid's hands snaked around my back in a slow caress. My fingers combed through her hair as I deepened the kiss. With the other hand, I untied the lace at the back of her dress, then slipped my hand between the parted sides. Her skin was warm and silky. She shuddered against me.

I loved that, despite her innocence, Astrid was embracing her sensuality and surrendering to my touch. There was no greater turn off than a cowering virgin. I had too little time with my brides to spend it coaxing them out of their virtuous fears. Rudeness or lack of etiquette did not dictate my forwardness in the ballroom. It was a good test as to how squeamish the maiden was. I had been down that road too many times.

Breaking the kiss, I gently pulled on her hair to expose her neck. My lips brushed alongside her throat, then nipped at the pulse there. She moaned, gripping my hair with both hands. I inhaled her scent, a delectable aroma all her own mixed with lavender. Astrid squeaked in surprise when she felt her dress slide down to pool at her feet. She instinctively tried to cover her nudity, but I would have none of that. Grabbing her hands, I held them behind her back. The restraining hold put her breasts on display for me, and I greedily sucked a dusky nipple into my mouth.

"Erik…" she moaned, pushing her chest forward.

My triumphant smile at her heady response couldn't be helped. I wanted her mad with desire for me, as I was for her.

As soon as I released her hands, she buried them in my hair again, holding me to her breasts. I licked, sucked, and nipped at each one in turn. Having untied the lace of her undergarments, I only released her long enough to get rid of the annoying obstruction. I recaptured Astrid's lips before she could become self-conscious about her now complete state of undress. Lifting her in my arms without breaking the kiss, I sat her at the edge of the bed and pushed her down against the mattress.

Kissing my way back down, I stopped briefly at her ample

but perky breasts before continuing my journey south. While my hands caressed and gently pinched her hard nipples, my mouth peppered soft kisses on her stomach and licked at her navel. Astrid's stomach quivered, and she squirmed beneath me. The musky scent of her arousal made me ache to taste her. Unable to resist, I got on my knees in front of the bed and spread her thighs before settling between them. She was beautiful. Her plump, pink cleft, surrounded by soft golden curls, already glistened for me.

"Erik! What are you doing?!"

Astrid tried to sit up and close her legs, embarrassed to be so exposed. However, I was too comfortably lodged between her legs, preventing her from hiding her womanly treasure from me. Pressing a hand on her stomach, I pushed her back down while my mouth latched onto the greatest of feasts. Whatever argument she intended to voice died in the moan that tore out of her. Her back arched off the bed, her hand gripping my hair almost painfully. There was no room, no time for shyness between us. I would teach her to be wild, wanton, and assertive in her desires.

My bride was dripping wet, writhing in pleasure under my tongue's frenzied assault. The sounds she made with that breathy, sultry voice of hers had my cock jerking in response. The way she said my name, full of need and hunger, made me want to keep her riding the edge of bliss until she begged me for release. When I slipped a finger inside her, with my tongue teasing her clitoris, Astrid's legs trembled, and her stomach quivered. Her reactions to my touch were intoxicating. I felt powerful, masterful, playing her luscious body like a fine-tuned instrument. I could go on for hours simply to watch her shuddering in ecstasy beneath my hands.

Astrid's labored breath and tortured moans told me she was close to completion. That was fine. I intended to give her many orgasms tonight, and I needed to prepare her to receive my considerable girth.

She seemed comfortable with one finger slipping in and out of her, so I added a second. It was a tighter fit, but her pelvis gyrating in counterpoint to my ministrations told me she was enjoying it. I couldn't wait for her to squirm like this, but with my cock inside her. Sucking even harder on her engorged little nub, I accelerated the movement of my fingers dipping into her, then curled them up, grazing the sensitive spot inside of her. Astrid shouted my name and arched her back so violently with pleasure that she nearly launched herself off the bed. That sent another blast of fiery lust down my spine. My testicles felt heavy, and my shaft throbbed with the need to claim her.

Her hands clawed at the mattress, and her head rolled from side to side as pleasure built within her. Astrid screamed, her body shaking with the spasms of bliss. She was so beautiful in her rapture, I had to clamp a tight hand around the base of my cock to keep myself from climaxing, too. My stomach cramped with the need for release, and I gritted my teeth through the burning ache. Only once buried balls deep inside my wife would I spill my seed. However, the urge to come didn't slow me down. While Astrid was riding out the waves of ecstasy, I scissored my fingers in and out of her, stretching her. I added a third finger which met with some resistance. Astrid didn't fight the intrusion, either too dazed to notice or the discomfort was negligible.

Looking up from my succulent feast, I took in the voluptuous beauty lying before me. Her amber darkened with passion. Her plump lips, slightly agape, emitted the sexiest keening sounds in response to my touch. Astrid's delicate hands plucked away at her hardened nipples, and my mouth watered, wanting to take their place. Under the candlelight, a thin coat of sweat on her honeyed skin made her glow. I wanted to lick every inch of her, and rub myself against her, skin to skin. Her legs shook with her impending release. I teased her sensitive spot a few more times, and she detonated once again.

Rising up, I slowly licked her tart essence from my hand, a

smug smile on my face. She tasted good, and her delicate musk was a heady aphrodisiac. Astrid looked at me with smoldering eyes, her breathing still labored. It caught in her throat when, after discarding my boots, I rid myself of my breeches. I wasn't a small man and towered by a full head above her. But it was the girth of my manhood that concerned her. Even with her prepared to receive me, it would be a tight fit. Her pleasure was all that mattered to me, though. I would go however slowly was required to avoid hurting her.

No woman had ever stirred such burning desire in me. From the moment my eyes noticed the golden goddess in the ballroom, my body clamored for her.

"Move up the bed, Astrid," I said, my voice thick with lust.

She scrambled backward eagerly. I suspected it was more to put distance between herself and my turgid shaft than out of docile obedience.

"Spread your legs for me," I said, crawling on top of the bed towards her.

After a slight hesitation, she complied. Her apprehension was palpable. To have her at my mercy, submitting to my will in spite of her fear, was incredibly intoxicating. Settling between her thighs, I lowered my chest to hers while supporting my weight on my forearms.

"Do not fear, my bride. I have no desire to harm you," I whispered, my lips inches from hers. "Pleasure is all I want to give you. Let me show you how good it can be between us."

Astrid nodded, giving me a shaky smile. That display of courage increased my respect for her. She would need every ounce of that strength to face the year that awaited her. I kissed her deeply, and she wrapped her arms around me, caressing my back. My wife's fluttering touches were electric, setting my skin ablaze. I would never get enough of that. My hand explored her body while our tongues continued to war. When the tension finally bled out of her, I started rubbing my cock against her soaking cleft, coating it with her essence. Astrid moaned and trembled every time the engorged head grazed her clitoris. The need to claim her was overwhelming, even if I only got to have her for a short while.

I shut out thoughts of the past, the future, of everything apart from giving into the moment and my burning desire. Placing the tip of my shaft against her opening, I gently pushed myself inside her. She was incredibly tight, so I got no further than the head of my cock before pulling out and pushing back in.

It took every ounce of my willpower to patiently rock in and out, gaining one excruciatingly slow inch after the other. She gasped against my mouth when I sank in deeper, and her nails dug into my back. I moaned at the sting and fought the urge to ram my cock the rest of the way in. I continued rocking slowly in and out of her and soon I was sheathed to the hilt.

"Astrid... You are so soft, so warm. Do you have any idea how good you feel around me?" I whispered, my voice hoarse with lust. "You were made for me."

I started pumping into her, half mad with pleasure. Each stroking motion sent bolts of liquid fire through my groin and exploded in blistering tendrils along my spine. She was so hot, so wet. The way her silky walls caressed my cock made me want to spill my seed. She felt so good... so damn good. And that sultry voice of hers...

"Are you mine, Astrid?"

"Yes... I... I'm yours... Oh Gods!"

When my cock once again hit her special spot, Astrid raked her nails down my back, and a strangled cry escaped me at the exquisite burn. I lost control. Lifting her leg to open her wider for me, I pounded into her. The slapping sound of skin meeting skin permeated the room. The need to come was riding me too hard; there was no more holding off. But I wanted her right there, with me.

My hand snaked between us, and I rubbed the swollen nub

between her legs. Moments later, she shattered into another orgasm. Her inner walls clamped down almost painfully around me. Gripping her hips in a bruising hold, I rammed my cock deep inside her and roared as blinding bliss streamed through my shaft. I held still for a few seconds while my seed filled her. The involuntary contractions of her sheath drained me to the last drop.

Shuddering from the vestiges of this glorious oblivion, I covered her face with soft kisses before rolling onto my back. I drew her into my embrace, and she snuggled close, her head resting on my shoulder. My heart hammered, and my labored breath echoed hers. I couldn't recall ever climaxing so hard nor sex ever feeling this good.

Full of wonder, I gazed at her lovely face, before running my hand down her back. It was slick with sweat, and she shivered. I vowed to make tomorrow, and the rest of her short life as easy and pleasurable as I could. But tonight, it was just us, and I reveled in every second of her blissful ignorance. Pulling the covers over us, I gave her one last sensuous kiss before we drifted off to sleep.

When we arose the next morning, the servants had already prepared a warm bath for us, which we made quick use of. Efficient as ever, Tormund had brought back some of Astrid's clothes and personal belongings after delivering the handfasting contract and bride token to her father. It pleased me to find out she favored flowy tunic dresses to the more elaborate, corseted gowns that many ladies wore. Tunic dresses were easier to remove and offered less protection against wandering hands. *My* hands…

Twice more last night, I had woken Astrid and made her mine. I would have done so again this morning if the first wedge of her medallion lighting up hadn't doused the burning embers of my arousal. Astrid hadn't noticed, but I couldn't postpone the inevitable. It was stupid of me to have allowed myself to think of us as merely husband and wife, even if only for one night. She would be dead in the next few weeks… or a handful of months, at best. However mind-blowing the sex had been, she was just a shooting star, briefly illuminating the endless darkness of my miserable life. I knew better than to get attached or let myself feel.

We engaged in casual chatter over breakfast. Our conversation was strained because of the tension building within her. She wanted to know what temptation would be set before her, and I had delayed enough.

"Are you ready?" I asked, when she pushed back her plate, sated.

Astrid didn't ask for what—there was no need. She answered with a stiff nod. I offered her my arm before leading her through the castle to the large doors blocking the entrance to the dungeon. On our way, we encountered a few servants scurrying about. Those who could gave us a wide berth, the others curtseyed before making a quick retreat.

"They're avoiding us," she whispered to herself.

Once again, my new bride's observational skills impressed me.

"Yes, they are."

She frowned and looked at me with questioning eyes. "But why?"

"Actually, they're avoiding *you*, to be more accurate."

Astrid's face took on a hurt expression, but she needed to understand the seriousness of her situation.

"It appears you were well-loved by your former servants. Until they know that you will succeed where others have failed, our servants would rather not grow fond of you."

She flinched but didn't comment. Her eyes glimmered with

determination, and she lifted her chin in defiance. I repressed a smile of approval. She would need this kind of attitude if she were to prevail. I opened the door to the dungeon. The air was damp and stuffy. Astrid moved closer to my side as we climbed down the narrow staircase. The flicker of the sconces along its sides, and the dripping sounds in the distance, made our descent even more ominous.

A short corridor at the base of the stairs opened up to an octagonal room. Multiple archways marked the paths to the various rooms within. But it was the closed arched door straight ahead that caught Astrid's attention. With a sound of awe, she left my side, walking ahead towards it.

My heart sank. Would she fail that quickly? She stood gaping at the large door. Its center bored a recessed keyhole in a shape matching her nautilus medallion. Intricate carvings resembling vine-like tendrils adorned the door's face. Each tendril spread from the keyhole and connected to one of twelve large gems embedded in the stone wall around the doorframe. Astrid ran her fingers along the carved patterns on the door.

"This is so beautiful! How does it open? What's inside?" she asked, turning to face me.

Her excitement faded when she noticed my stern expression. She frowned, glanced at the door, then back at me. Her eyes widened in understanding, and she quickly backed away from it.

"Is this it?" she asked, looking warily at the door. "Is that the temptation?"

"Yes," I said, standing right in front of the bane of my existence. I ran a hand over the door before facing my wife. "You must never open that door, Astrid. Never. Do not ever seek to find out what lies within. And never, ever, under any circumstances, enter the room beyond of your own free will. Do you understand what I'm saying?"

"Yes, Erik." She nodded frantically, still casting worried glances at the door.

"I would have your solemn word on this, Astrid," I said, cupping her face with both hands. "Swear it to me. Swear by all that you hold dear that you will never open this door, and that you will never go inside. Swear it."

"I swear it, Erik." She put her trembling hands on my chest. "With the Gods as my witnesses, I swear it. I will never open this door, and I will never go inside."

Drawing her to me, I crushed her lips with mine. The kiss was more desperate than passionate. Twenty-seven times before I'd heard such a promise. Twenty-seven times it had been broken. I didn't want to care for Astrid: I couldn't afford to. But I feared I was already starting to.

She looked at the door once more and suddenly pulled out the necklace hidden beneath her tunic dress. "That's the key," she said to me. When I nodded, she asked, "If breaking the curse requires your wife not to open the door for one year, why show it to me? Why give me the key and set me up for possible failure?"

"Because it is in the nature of curses to set a challenge nigh impossible to overcome. You cannot break a curse by simply hiding from it. It's meant to test you to your limits, ensuring most will fail." I took the medallion from her hands. "But in this instance, there's another reason I must show this to you." I flipped the medallion around. "Notice anything different?"

Thirty-one segments divided the spiraled pattern of the nautilus: one for each day of the current month—Mars.

"The first segment, at the base of the spiral... It wasn't lit before," she said.

"Correct. Every day that you wear it, another segment will light up. Once all of them are lit, you must place the medallion in the keyhole and turn it counterclockwise to transfer the energy to them," I said pointing at the gems embedded in the stone wall. "You will repeat this twelve times. Succeed, and all this ends."

"This energy... The medallion isn't sucking out my soul or anything, is it?"

"No, Astrid. As I told you, the medallion isn't meant to harm you."

"Ok then," she said with a relieved sigh. "This sounds straightforward enough. I should be able to handle that."

I gave her a sad smile. "For both our sakes, I hope you can."

CHAPTER 4
ASTRID

E rik gave me a tour of the open sections of the castle. Most of them were devoted to his royal functions. The throne room and the council chamber were where he spent most of his time. There was a boudoir for me to use at my leisure and one of the most impressive private libraries I had ever seen. While many of the topics of the books themselves didn't inspire me, their craftsmanship and the beautiful illuminations alone kept me coming back. We rarely used the ballroom, but the adjoining music room would become one of my favorite places in the castle. Although I was proficient with the flute and harpsichord, it was the harp I loved the most. I spent many evenings with Erik sipping rum while he listened to me playing.

In light of Erik's comment, I avoided the servants. While I had no intentions of failing, making them uncomfortable or reading pity in their eyes was the last thing I needed or wanted. Erik had encouraged me to explore the castle and to have any room I desired reopened—no restriction other than the Sealed Door.

During the first couple of weeks, I followed his suggestion. Or rather, I did when I wasn't reading, embroidering, or writing letters to my sister. It was less scary in the light of day. However, the dusty, stuffy rooms and the covered furniture didn't exactly spur my enthusiasm. I would investigate a handful of rooms, then answer the call of the courtyard and its fabulous gardens.

In the end, it was the gallery that drove me out of the castle and snuffed out any desire to explore it further. An entire wall had been dedicated to Erik's past wives—twenty-seven in total. Next to Ariana's portrait—his last bride—a golden plaque read the name 'Astrid'.

I felt my blood drain from my face. Why did he already have my name up there? Was Erik so sure I would fail like the others? The challenge has been so easy so far. Was there something else he had hidden from me? Was he already tiring of me as his wife and counting the days until I failed?

As one horrible thought after the other filled my mind, the paintings seemed to come to life. Each ex-wife was glaring at me accusingly. But why would they? I had nothing to do with their demise. I blinked and shook my head, knowing this was only my imagination playing tricks on me.

However, I nearly jumped out of my skin when something akin to an evil woman's laughter suddenly resonated inside the room... No, not the room... Inside my head. It echoed loudly, malicious and taunting.

Overwhelmed by an impending sense of doom, I blindly ran out of the castle, not caring about the startled shouts and worried looks of the guards and servants. I couldn't breathe. I needed to get away. However, the burning in my lungs and legs eventually forced me to stop. Taking in my surroundings, I realized this was an abandoned section of the immense courtyard, deep beyond the gardens. In the distance, the castle loomed under the bright mid-afternoon sun.

A few feet from me, a broken fountain stood amidst over-grown vegetation. I sat by the edge to catch my breath. It was silly of me to have overreacted like that. There had been no laughter. My overactive imagination was playing tricks on me.

I looked at my makeshift bench. Moss and vines had claimed what had surely been a beautiful piece of art. In the middle of the fountain, the life-sized statue of a crowned mermaid sat on the back of a white horse with a fishtail. Her dead eyes also seemed to stare at me. Feeling uneasy, I got up and walked away.

The air was fresh and delicately scented by the surrounding wildflowers. The sun felt like a warm caress on my face. My sister Kara would chastise me for exposing myself like this. Among my many shortcomings, my olive skin was a far cry from the fair complexion believed to be the epitome of beauty. My propensity to seek the outdoors and walk in the sun did nothing to improve my situation—not that I particularly cared.

I followed a stone path hidden by bushy trees and overgrowth. I wondered where it led, and why they had let nature reclaim this area. It wasn't long before I stumbled upon an abandoned greenhouse. Why they built it so far from the castle was a mystery. Although the door wasn't locked, it took a bit of effort to open. The rusty hinges resisted and complained, but eventually yielded to my persistence.

The potent smell of wet earth and rotting leaves greeted me. Dead potted plants and dust covered two long tables. More pots hung from metal poles along the glass ceiling. Against the back wall, a pair of faded cast-iron chairs sat near a workbench with various gardening tools and containers. I picked up one of the sealed containers and shook it gently. It sounded like there were seeds inside. I opened the side drawers of the workbench. One was empty, and the other contained more gardening tools. The third was locked. Intrigued, I looked for the key—in vain.

Disappointed, I explored the vicinity of the greenhouse. It would require work, but it could be restored to its former glory. Blocking out the knowledge that it had no doubt belonged to one of Erik's previous wives, I started making plans for my new botanical retreat.

A few hours later, I decided it was time to return to the castle. The sun would set soon, and I didn't want to walk through the underbrush in the dark.

Tormund greeted me at the entrance with an air of obvious relief.

"Your Highness, I'm pleased to see you're well. We were worried."

"Oh? I'm sorry if I caused you any distress. But why the concern?"

"The servants saw you running out of the castle, apparently upset. You were gone for hours. Is everything all right?"

My hysterical reaction to those portraits was embarrassing and best forgotten. I nodded with a smile I hoped would reassure him.

"Yes, Master Tormund. All is well. I needed a little fresh air."

He seemed to want to press the issue but, after a brief hesitation, he offered me his arm instead. "Dinner will be served shortly. I will take you to the dining hall. His Majesty will join you presently."

Accepting his arm, I followed him in silence, wishing I had returned earlier to freshen up. While I took reasonable care of my appearance, I had never been particularly coquettish—until now. The way Erik looked at me, silver eyes stormy with desire, did the most delicious things to me. He hadn't lied that first night, a fortnight ago, when he hinted at the extent of his sexual appetite. My husband was insatiable... and I loved it.

Erik met us as we reached the dining hall. Tormund bowed and retreated while Erik escorted me to my chair. The look on his face told me he had heard of my escapade, and it worried him. A pair of servants laid a meal of braised venison, boiled vegetables, and fresh bread on the table. They served us wine and left a full jug near Erik before discreetly exiting.

Erik raised his glass to me, and I returned the gesture. We both drank before tucking into the perfectly seasoned food.

"How has your day been, Astrid?" The intensity of his gaze belied his casual tone.

"It has been... interesting," I said, non-committal.

"I hear you were upset."

Pushing the vegetables around my plate with my fork, I pondered whether to be truthful about what had driven me out in a state of panic.

"Are you having... difficulties?"

His words and the tension in his voice made me realize he feared I was already failing.

"No, Erik. I'm not feeling any compulsion to break my oath."

And I truly didn't. Aside from a mild curiosity, I didn't have the slightest urge to approach the Sealed Door. Erik's eyes flicked between mine, assessing the truthfulness of my words. I held his gaze without flinching. After a moment, he blinked, and the tension seemed to bleed out of him.

"Good, good... So why did you run away?"

"I saw my name in the gallery."

The silence that settled between us was thick and uneasy. With an unreadable expression on his face, Erik drained his glass of wine, and then refilled it from the jug.

"It is only a name, Astrid."

"One of many," I said. He frowned at my words. "But rest assured, Erik, I intend for it to be the last."

A strange expression crossed his features. "Nothing would please me more, Astrid. Remain steadfast in your promise, and so it shall be."

I nodded. We continued eating quietly for a while. Breaking the silence, I told him about the abandoned greenhouse. To my surprise, he didn't object when I asked to restore it.

"Ask Tormund for anything you want done. He will have the servants perform the work to your specifications."

"Actually, I would rather do it myself," I said. "The only help I need is for someone to replace the rusty door and clear the overgrown path leading to it."

His raised eyebrow told me that my answer took him aback. "As you wish." Pushing his plate back, he reclined in his chair. "Will you play the harp again for me tonight?"

My face heated with pleasure. "Of course, Erik. I would be delighted."

~

Morning found Erik in an even stranger mood than last night. At his request, I played the harp for nearly two hours. His eyes never left me, as if he was trying to memorize my features. It had been... uncanny. When he finally seemed satisfied, he carried me to our room and made love to me with an intensity that bordered on desperation. It went on for hours. While it had been amazing, I couldn't deny the soreness I now felt.

Even now, he was finishing dressing with a pensive, if not troubled expression. Unable to withstand the uneasiness any longer, I confronted him.

"What's wrong, Erik? You're acting strange."

"I have to go away for a while," he said, his voice impassive.

"Oh... When will you leave? And how long will you be gone?"

"Within the hour. I will be gone a fortnight."

That hit me in the gut. I clutched my chest in shock. My distress was due to far more than just losing my only real companion. Obviously, I would miss him. But with Erik gone, I would be completely alone in the castle every night for the next two weeks. I shook my head in denial.

"You can't leave me all by myself. Take me with you."

He clenched his jaw, and his gaze hardened. "I can't take you."

"Why not? I will make myself scarce. You won't even notice I'm there."

"No, Astrid. I cannot take you because you cannot leave the castle's grounds. Not until the year is up."

I backed away from him, wrapping my arms around my midsection. "What are you saying? Am I a prisoner?"

"In a manner of speaking, I guess you are," he said.

As if unable to withstand my disbelieving stare, Erik turned away from me and stood by the fireplace.

"The medallion cannot leave the realm without dire consequences," he explained, looking into the dying embers. "And you cannot part with it without incurring dreadful repercussions. In theory, you could go as far as the city of Revna for a few hours, but no longer before you would need to return. The medallion should ideally never leave the castle's grounds."

Erik faced me, his expression a mixture of sadness and guilt.

"The property is vast. You won't feel confined. If ever the medallion pulses pink, you must return to the castle at once."

"But I will be completely alone, Erik! What if something happens to me during the night?"

Erik emitted a growling sound, like an enraged beast. He marched up to me and held my head in an iron grip. "Nothing will happen to you, do you hear me?" he said through gritted teeth. "Nothing... You will lock yourself in our room every night and go to sleep. Nothing and no one can get inside the castle without a guard catching them. You're safe. Be true to your word, and all will be well. It's only a few days, and I will return to you."

I put my hands on his muscular chest. My eyes flicked

36

between his, searching. "But can't someone come stay with me in your absence? I don't want to be alone in the castle. I'm scared."

He shook his head again, and my heart sank even deeper. "You can have guests during the day, but they must be gone by nightfall. For their sake and yours."

A sharp knock on our bedroom door startled me. Erik sighed and rested his forehead on mine.

"It's only a few days, Astrid. Be true, and I will return to you. Be strong."

I wanted to argue, but he silenced me with a passionate kiss before walking out. Running after him, I shouted his name outside our bedroom door. He didn't turn back and kept on walking with Tormund shadowing him.

Pressing my forehead against the doorframe, I wept.

E ven with the servants buzzing about during the day, I couldn't stand staying within the castle. I devoted every waking moment to restoring the greenhouse while dreading the oppressive silence that awaited me come nightfall. The first three nights were the worst, despite Tormund's best efforts to reassure me. In the evening, he had the servants light every candle, chandelier, and candelabra along any area of the castle I might cross or enter during the night. They would continue to burn until the servants put them out in the morning. It was a tremendous waste, and I felt guilty for squandering resources like that. But there was no way I would dwell within the deserted castle with the terrifying shadows closing in around me.

I locked the door to my room and wedged a chair under the handle. Lying in bed, my mind became my worst enemy. It conjured fantastic monsters lurking outside my door, transformed the faintest sound into demonic whispers, and every object or shadow into hellish beasts on a mission to steal my soul.

The crackling sound of a burning log crumbling in the fireplace awoke me with a start. Realizing I had somehow managed to doze off, my eyes darted to the door to ensure the chair was still safely wedged there. It was. The dim light provided by the fireplace allowed me to somewhat make out the shape of some of the decorative items on the dresser across from the bed. One looked like a human head facing me.

The more I stared at it, the more defined it became. I knew it was just my imagination playing tricks on me, but the pounding of my heart wouldn't let the matter rest. Getting out of bed—my eyes never leaving the 'head'—I grabbed the candleholder on my nightstand and warily approached the object of my fears. It was an ornate vase. Feeling like an idiot, I returned to bed.

Moments later, despite knowing it was just a vase, my eyes kept flicking back to it. With an aggravated groan, I got back up, grabbed the vase, and hid it in the closet. On my way back to bed, I paused, picked up a chair, and wedged it under the closet door. Sleep didn't come quickly after that, but I felt better. I would need to put the vase back in its place in the morning though, to avoid any awkward explanation to the servants.

The next two nights were a repeat of the first. The fourth night though, the strangest thing happened. I woke up to find a beautiful woman with long blond hair sitting on the couch in front of the fireplace. How she had gotten inside my bedroom with the chair still wedged under the door handle was a mystery. Her presence should have scared me, but for some reason it didn't. I sat up in my bed, my eyes never leaving the intruder.

"Ah, you're finally awake," the woman said.

"Who are you, and what are you doing in my room?"

"My name is Traxia, and I'm a friend."

Traxia wore a servant's uniform, but I didn't recall ever

seeing such a beauty among the staff. I pulled down the blankets and sat at the edge of the bed.

"What do you want?" I asked, tension seeping into my voice. "You shouldn't be here after nightfall. It isn't safe."

"You're right, your Highness, but this was my only chance to speak to you away from prying eyes and ears," Traxia said. "I have a proposal for you that could be highly beneficial to both of us."

I immediately became suspicious. "What kind of proposal?"

"I know where to find some of the lost treasures from the merchant and trade ships that sank during the years the kraken threatened our shores," Traxia said, her eyes sparkling with excitement. "Together, we could retrieve it and split the bounty. There's a fortune to be had."

"Why would you tell me this? If there's such wealth lying about, why not keep it to yourself?" I didn't hide the skepticism in my tone.

"Your wariness is both wise and understandable, your Highness," Traxia said in a conciliatory tone. "I would no doubt react the same. The reason I confide this to you is that the only way to access it is through the dungeons. The guards will become suspicious if I go there by myself during the day, and I'm not supposed to be in the castle at night."

"You could have told King Erik about this and claim finder's reward," I said, still feeling uneasy about the woman.

Traxia snorted. "Finder's fee would put food on the table for a few months at best. The full treasure will have my family set in a life of luxury for generations."

She rose from the couch and took a couple of steps towards me. I tensed and stood up from the bed to be in a less vulnerable position.

"With your share, your family would never have to worry about their finances anymore. Your bride token only kept your father and sister from becoming destitute. But still, your sister needs to accept the first decent proposal she gets or end up living hand-to-mouth within the next few years."

Her assessment was right. I didn't know the amount of the bride token, but that money would need to be spent sparingly until my sister Kara found herself a good husband. It was a tempting offer, but something about Traxia rubbed me the wrong way.

"How did you get past the guards? No one is allowed into the castle after sunset."

She gave me a blank stare. "I hid inside the castle when everyone left. But…"

I pointed at the chair still jamming the handle. "How did you get inside my room with the door blocked?"

"What does it matter?" Traxia snapped. "We need to go get that treasure. I won't have another chance to do this. So can we—"

"No. We can't. I want you out of my room this instant." I walked towards the cord to ring the bell which would summon the guards.

"You stupid cow," Traxia snarled before launching herself at me.

I took a step back and raised my hands in protection. In my haste, I tripped and felt myself falling. My scream startled me awake. Heart pounding, it took me a while to realize it had only been a dream. I didn't sleep for the rest of the night.

That morning, I was beyond exhausted and ended up sleeping half the day. It was early afternoon when I finally got up. After a quick breakfast-lunch, I headed to the greenhouse, berating myself the whole way there. My irrational fears were driving me insane, and it was time to put an end to it. Three nights and nothing had happened other than keeping myself up in a frenzied state. I vowed to chase any silly thoughts from my mind. Failing that, I would busy myself reading or embroidering rather than succumbing to wild imaginings.

The workers assigned to the greenhouse by Tormund had done a wonderful job of clearing the path and overgrowth. They had replaced the rusty door with a shiny new one, and the glass walls and ceiling were gleaming. Brand new pots and gardening tools lay atop the workbench. I was eager to discover what plants would sprout from the seeds in the sealed containers. I grabbed some fresh dirt from the cart outside and went to work.

An hour into it, I turned to take the trowel from the work-bench. The locked drawer drew my attention when the reflection of the sun glimmered on its golden handle. Curious as to what it might contain, I used my jeweled hairpin in the keyhole to force it open. I was about to give up when a sharp clicking sound announced my success. Shrieking with delight, I carefully pulled the drawer open. It creaked and squeaked, the wood having swollen from humidity and disuse. Inside lay the most unexpected treasure.

A golden locket hung at the end of a long, delicate gold chain. On one face of the locket, a mermaid with wavy hair and a crown curled her tail around a circular gem oddly similar to the one on my nautilus medallion. On the other face of the locket, there was a long-maned rearing horse with a fishtail. The fins of its tail constituted the locket's clasp. The mermaid and seahorse were clearly the same from the broken fountain.

Frowning, I opened the locket, and my breath caught in my throat as I gazed at the two miniature portraits inside. A beautiful woman with silver eyes, midnight blue hair, and a crown of corals and precious gems smiled on one side. On the other side, a man bearing an uncanny resemblance to Erik, except for his dark blond hair and blue eyes, stared back at me.

They weren't Erik's parents. His father, the late King Brandt Thorsen, had been brown-haired and green-eyed. When his black-haired and brown-eyed mother, Queen Dagmar, had given birth to Erik, many had questioned her faithfulness to her husband. Despite his unusual hair and eye coloring, Erik's likeness to King Brandt as he grew up soon quelled any doubt about his legitimacy.

His parents died eighteen years ago when a kraken attacked and sank their ship. It was the first time since a Thorsen had ascended the throne, over eighty years ago, that the seas had turned against us. In the four years following their deaths, the creature terrorized the fledgling kingdom of Rathlin Islands and nearly brought us to our knees. At age nineteen, Erik had sailed off to face the beast. Many good men died that day, but Erik returned triumphant... and cursed. It was unclear who cast the curse on him. Some say it was a sea witch who had considered the kraken her pet. We only knew that from that day forward, Erik had to be married, and his wife had one year to break the curse or die trying. Should he remain unwed for more than ninety days, the kraken would rise again.

And so, for the last fourteen years, he had watched wife after wife fail. Closing the locket, I resumed the long walk back to the castle, and vowed to myself that I would succeed.

CHAPTER 5
ERIK

The last two weeks put me through pure hell. I learned years ago that leaving my young bride by herself so early after our handfasting would likely result in tragedy. But I was the King of Rathlin Islands and couldn't shirk my diplomatic responsibilities, even for my bride. My Astrid…

I was starting to care for her more than wisdom dictated. The way I had left her a fortnight ago shamed me. To be honest, I had delayed informing her of my departure to grant her one last peaceful night… not that I actually allowed her to sleep. I should have delivered the news more gently, given her the chance to absorb and accept it. Instead, I had fled like a coward. Her distress had been unbearable, especially knowing it couldn't be helped.

Not for the first time, I wondered if I should have explained to her the nature of the evil that lurked beyond the Sealed Door. However, I had tried that before with a few of my previous brides, with catastrophic results. Some had shunned me once they found out about my true nature and fought the losing battle alone. Others, once they understood the threat, saw it everywhere, even where it wasn't. And when they didn't, they sought it out, making themselves more vulnerable to its lure.

Astrid was different from my previous brides; more perceptive, more focused, and incredibly strong beneath her gentle demeanor. Maybe she could handle the truth, but I didn't dare risk it.

Since my departure, every day, every hour, every minute, my eyes stared at the ring on my finger, dreading the moment its gem would announce Astrid's failure. But the iridescent gem thankfully retained its whitish glow. After the first week passed, I began to hope. On the thirteenth night, I stood vigil on the bridge as we sailed home on an oily sea, made darker by the moonless sky. We made good time and would be home one day early. It was only when the first rays of the rising sun burned on the horizon that I finally believed I wouldn't lose her—at least not yet.

The fierceness of my happiness left me perplexed. Obviously, I didn't want to be widowed once more... or ever again for that matter. But it was the thought of keeping Astrid specifically that made my heart soar. The strength of my attraction to her, the ravenous hunger she stirred within me baffled me. She didn't exactly fit my usual type.

I liked my women strikingly beautiful, tall, lean, and fair of hair and skin, sophisticated, bold, and fierce. Strangely, Hilda fit that profile perfectly, yet I couldn't stand her or the thought of touching her. While Astrid wasn't short, I towered over her by a full head. She wasn't a beauty, but her features were attractive. My new bride was deliciously plump, with silky, golden skin, luscious lips, full breasts, and the most perfect behind. Just thinking of her had blood rushing to my groin.

But her physical attributes weren't the only reason I was growing so fond of her. Although not as bold and outspoken as Hilda, Astrid didn't qualify as meek or timid. She possessed a quiet strength and a serene elegance, laced with fierce determina-

tion and unwavering loyalty to those she loved. Her understanding of the servants' reluctance to bond with her, and the
dauntless way she was facing the challenge impressed me.
Watching her play the harp for me was mesmerizing, and in a
few hours, I would get to experience that pleasure again.

As soon as we reached the shore, I hurried off the ship. I rode
my horse hard, eager to surprise Astrid with my early arrival.
Although baffled by my unusual haste, my guards followed
along in silence. As I reached the entrance of the castle, Tormund
raced down the stairs to meet me. Before I could dismount, he
informed me Astrid was in the greenhouse. I gestured for my
guards to stay and raced towards it. Once at the cleared path, I
dismounted, tied my horse to a tree and walked the remaining
distance.

Standing by the glass door, I observed my wife through the
window. Her lips moved, and I could faintly hear the melody she
sang. She wore a beige tunic dress with bronze and gold embroidery. Her blonde hair flowed freely down her back. I longed to
bury my face in its softness and inhale her lavender-scented
perfume. Astrid finished organizing the sprouting pots on one of
the tables, then took a step back to admire her work.

Only then did she finally notice me.

Startled, she pressed a hand to her chest, right below the
nautilus medallion that shone brightly with a pulsating glow. Her
stunned expression morphed into one of such raw happiness that
my heart tightened in my chest. I opened the door and marched
towards her. Astrid's eyes misted. Her lips formed the syllables
of my name though no sound escaped through them. She ran the
remaining distance and threw herself into my arms.

I crushed her lips with a bruising kiss. The fresh lavender
scent I had so missed filled my nostrils. I embraced her voluptuous body while my tongue invaded her mouth. She buried her
hands in my hair and gripped the strands almost painfully.
Moaning with pleasure, she pressed her chest against mine. My

hands slid down to her behind and held her tightly against my hardening shaft. Coming up for air, I covered her face with kisses.

"Erik, I need you," Astrid whispered, her voice raspy with desire.

"Astrid…" I moaned hungrily when she clawed at my clothes.

"I need you, Erik. Right now!"

She slipped her hands under my tunic and pulled the string of my breeches. Her face was flushed and her breathing labored. The raw glint in her amber eyes, darkened by desire, sent blistering pulses of lust through my shaft, driving me over the edge. I lifted her in my arms, and she wrapped her legs around my waist. Devouring her mouth in another passionate kiss, I carried her to the back of the greenhouse.

I stopped in front of the workbench and swiped my hand over its surface, throwing a few gardening tools and a watering can to the ground. The sound of metal hitting the floor and splashing water barely registered in my lust-crazed mind.

I sat Astrid at the edge of the workbench and pulled down the top of her dress to suck an erect nipple into my mouth. She whimpered with pleasure and struggled to lift the long skirt of her dress.

"I want you inside me, Erik. Now… Take me, now!"

Without stopping to suck and lick the succulent treat, I helped her raise her skirt. Astrid lifted her behind from the workbench to allow me to pull her undergarments off. Leaning back on her forearms, she placed her feet on top of the workbench, spreading herself wide open for me. I slipped two fingers into her opening while feverishly freeing my aching cock from the confines of my breeches. She was soaking wet.

Astrid shouted my name when my thumb grazed the swollen nub between her legs. That incredibly sultry voice of hers, the intoxicating scent of her musk, and the urgency with which she pulled at me drove me insane with need. I drew her hips to the edge of the bench and shoved my cock into her welcoming heat in one powerful thrust.

I pounded into her at a punishing pace. Our moans and shouts of pleasure couldn't fully drown out the creaking sound of the workbench under my frenzied assault, nor the clinking of the seed containers on top of it.

"Astrid... My Astrid... I missed you so much."

She screamed as she exploded around my cock. Her inner walls clamped down on my shaft, but I wasn't ready to climax—nowhere near. I still wanted her too much. While she rode the waves of her orgasm, I continued rocking back and forth inside her searing heat, laving her breasts with my tongue, and nipping at her nipples.

What a magnificent vision she was, her hair splayed about, her eyes glazed over, her lips swollen by my kisses. Even in the ebbing throes of her climax, the mere sight of her turned my blood to molten lava. When she seemed to have regained enough of her senses, I pulled out of her. After getting Astrid to her feet, I turned her around and bent her over the workbench. Burying my cock to the hilt, I slipped in and out of her with renewed vigor.

Astrid shouted my name, over and over again in a mantra. With her palms flat on the workbench, she arched back into me. I fondled her breast with one hand while the other slipped between her legs to rub her engorged clitoris. The crashing sound of glass shattering as one of the sealed containers fell off the workbench mingled with our gasps of pleasure.

Sweat dripped down my back from the exertion and the burning early afternoon sun through the glass ceiling. Astrid's legs began to shake, and I could feel her inner walls convulsing around my shaft. She was on the verge of another climax, and I would ride this one with her.

My movements became erratic as blistering coils of pleasure

unraveled within me. Astrid shouted and arched violently into me as she once more found her release. I hollered in response when my own orgasm overtook me. With my cock buried deep, I spilled my seed inside her in blissful pulses. I held her close, covering her neck and back with soft kisses.

She collapsed on top of the workbench, and I leaned over her, supporting my weight on my forearms on either side of her. Astrid turned her face to the side, and I nuzzled her cheek and neck. We savored the intimate embrace in silence, while catching our breaths. I eventually pulled out of her. Getting up, I tucked myself back into my breeches, and helped Astrid readjust her clothing.

"Wow," I said, looking at the disaster area we had created around the workbench.

"Welcome home," she whispered with a naughty smile.

Chuckling, I rubbed my nose against hers. "It is good to be home."

The absence of Astrid's warm body against mine woke me up. She was sitting on the couch in front of the fireplace, staring blindly at the dying embers within. Her fingers absent-mindedly toyed with the nautilus medallion hanging from her necklace. Now fully charged, it glowed like a miniature sun. Frowning, I sat up and wondered what somber thoughts had driven her from our bed. The motion snapped her out of her musing. She turned to face me. The serene expression on her face alleviated some of my fears.

"Hey," she said with a gentle smile.

"Hey," I said, smiling back. Getting out of bed, I went to sit beside her. "Is everything all right?"

Nodding, Astrid snuggled against me. She lifted the medallion, showing it to me. "It's shining so bright, it woke me up. I guess it's ready now?"

"Yes, my darling," I said with a soft voice. "You have completed the first month. Before nightfall, you will need to activate the first seal."

"Can we do it now and get this out of the way? I don't want to spend an entire day anxiously awaiting the moment I'll have to touch that door again."

"Absolutely, Astrid. Whatever makes you feel most comfortable." I caressed her silky hair and placed a gentle kiss on her temple.

We got dressed quietly then headed to the dungeon. Our footsteps echoed in the empty hallways since the servants hadn't arrived yet. However, the silence wasn't ominous. The rising sun was still low on the horizon, and with it, a sense of peace— hope?—settled over me. I stole a glance at Astrid. She walked purposefully, a look of determination on her pretty face.

Pride and gratitude blossomed in my heart. With most of my previous wives, this first seal had been a trial in and of itself. It forced them to interact with the very object that they were otherwise bound to avoid at the peril of their lives.

Temptation had ensnared some of my previous wives from the moment they saw the necklace and heard of the door. Most of the others started showing the first signs of weakness to its lure by the second week. In the entire month since her arrival, Astrid had felt no compulsion, not even during the nights she was completely alone in the castle. I didn't want to read more into it than there was, but my mind had a will of its own.

We climbed down the dungeon's stairs and made our way to the Sealed Door. Astrid stopped a couple of feet in front of it and turned to me for guidance. I approached her and indicated the face of the medallion with the pulsating gem.

"You must place the medallion here," I said, pointing at the nautilus-shaped recess in the door. "The gemmed side must face inward, then you turn it counterclockwise. Remember, *always* to the left. Turning it clockwise means death. It would release the seals and open the door."

Astrid shuddered at my words and swallowed hard. With a stiff nod, she turned to face the door. She couldn't hide the slight trembling of her hand as she raised it to place the medallion in the socket, but she didn't falter. A soft gasp escaped her when a shimmering glow pulsated for a couple of seconds along the vine-like carvings on the face of the door, then faded away.

Astrid licked her lips nervously then rotated the medallion as per my instructions. The lowest carved tendril that sprouted from the socket to the left side of the door slowly filled with a silver light. It bled over the doorframe and into the bottom seal embedded in the stone wall around the door.

The first seal came to life, filling with light as it absorbed the medallion's energy. Astrid groaned, as if in pain. Suddenly unsteady on her legs, she slapped a hand on the face of the door to support herself. I watched helplessly as Astrid rested her forehead on the door with a whimper and started panting. Though her knuckles were white, and her hand now visibly shook, she still firmly held the medallion in place in the socket. At last, a blinding glow and a hollow clicking sound indicated the transfer was complete.

She had fully activated the first seal.

Astrid heaved a sigh of relief and nearly collapsed against the door. Now that the process had ended, I could finally wrap my arms around her in support. She leaned against me. The expression on her face was a mix of exhaustion and gratitude.

"It's done, my darling." I softly kissed her brow. "You can remove the medallion."

She nodded groggily and removed the nautilus from the socket. I picked her up in my arms, and Astrid curled into me, almost in a fetal position, her face buried in my neck. With one last look at the Sealed Door, I turned around and headed for the stairs out of the dungeon.

Tormund stood on the landing, a concerned look on his face. I gave him a reassuring smile, and he relaxed. A quick glance at the now dim medallion resting on Astrid's chest provided him with all the confirmation he needed. Tormund gave me a short bow before moving out of the way, but his eyes had been on Astrid's face. In truth, it was her he was thanking.

Brushing past him, and under the curious, but discreet stares of the servants who had begun trickling in to work, I took my bride back to our room.

CHAPTER 6
ASTRID

Two weeks after activating that first seal, I was finally leaving the prison that the castle had become for me. After much coaxing and pleading through the letters I'd been exchanging with my sister, I'd finally convinced Kara to meet me for tea in town. Despite his obvious reluctance, Tormund had assigned a couple of guards to escort my carriage.

I hated leaving without telling Erik. He'd left early that morning for some official visit to a neighboring town. Granted, I'd informed him of my efforts to meet with my sister, but as our father had forbidden her to come to the castle, we'd come up with a workaround. Kara had to find the perfect opportunity to make it look like we 'accidentally' ran into each other without Father nearby, for fear he would take her away at once.

The note had arrived barely three hours after Erik's departure, enjoining me to meet her at the modiste in town. I wasted no time. After switching my casual dress into something more suited to my station, I jumped into the carriage and headed to the city of Revna. According to my husband, I couldn't stay away more than four hours from the castle grounds. Considering it was a forty-minute carriage ride in each direction, I would have a measly two hours with my sister. But it was better than nothing.

I also looked forward to being surrounded by people again, seeing familiar faces instead of the distant servants scurrying about. A part of me wanted to make a brief detour to see Father Osvald. But with so little time with my sister, it didn't feel reasonable.

My heart soared as the silhouette of the tall wood and stone buildings of Revna started rising on the horizon. Soon, the clobbering of countless horse hooves on the paved roads and the grinding of chariot wheels filled the air, accompanied by the hum of multiple voices. A grin settled on my face upon hearing merchants loudly calling out to passersby to lure them to their stalls or shops. To think it used to annoy me. Now I could listen to them all day.

I leaned forward in my seat to look out the window and feast my eyes on the familiar scenery. Far too many people still crowded the streets. The same storefronts desperately required a fresh coat of paint, while others could really use a dose or two— or ten—of humility and simplicity. The same delectable aromas wafted to me as we neared one of Revna's largest bakeries. I would have to grab a few treats on my way back.

The way I took everything in, you'd think I'd been 'trapped' inside the castle for a year rather than a month and a half. But I'd learned the hard way that we took far too many things for granted. It was only once you had lost something that you truly appreciated its value.

In my excitement, it took me a moment to notice the shift in the city's mood. All that enthusiastic activity and noise had gradually dampened to a curious hush as more and more people realized what carriage had just rolled into town. My stomach knotted as many conversations stopped, every eye locked on my vehicle, some people pointing in my direction and leaning in to whisper to their friends.

I slumped back against my seat, my joy doused by a reaction that I should have expected. I'd always prided myself on being observant, a great judge of character, and having a pretty good intuition when it came to how people behaved. However, the past few weeks living in the castle appeared to have made me lean more towards wishful thinking than reality.

Although, to be fair, I couldn't fully blame people's change of attitude on the curse weighing over me. I was the Queen now, and they were my subjects. For that alone, they would no longer casually approach me or talk to me like they once did.

I chose to make that the reason for the hush.

My carriage came to a stop in front of Tora's boutique. My heart warmed at the thought Kara could finally refresh her wardrobe at the establishment of one of the finest seamstresses in Rathlin. It had been years since we'd been able to afford new clothes—or anything else for that matter.

But where others had fully shunned us during our times of hardship, Tora had still consented to mend and modify some of our outfits to give them a second life. It pleased me tremendously that Kara repaid that kindness with properly paid patronage now that our family's finances had bounced back.

A guard opened the carriage's door to help me down. I didn't shy away from the gawkers. Making eye contact with those who had gravitated near the boutique to get a closer look at me, I smiled and nodded at the crowd in a way that hopefully came across as friendly but regal. Above all, I wanted them to see that the curse held no power over me. Judging by the surprised—and even impressed—looks on many faces, I wanted to believe I had succeeded. In all the ways that mattered, this was a psychological war.

The doors of the boutique opened long before I reached it. Tora, a plump little brunette in her late forties, multiplied the bows and curtsies as she waved me in.

"Your Majesty honors my humble boutique with your presence. Please! Please, do come in. Your sister is already inside for some fittings," Tora said, her voice bubbling with excitement.

"Thank you, Tora," I said gently. "It is a pleasure to see you again."

One guard entered for a quick inspection inside, mainly at the main area where various mannequins displayed fancy dresses and shelves boasted rolls of the most luxurious and exotic fabrics. He left almost immediately to grant us privacy.

Where monarchs in many other countries often needed heavy protection for fear of those who would try to assassinate them, I certainly had no such fear in Rathlin. The citizens wouldn't wish me any harm. My survival meant theirs and peace for the realm.

But such thoughts faded from my mind as soon as Tora led me through the boutique to one of two private salons at the back. The door parted to reveal my sister, looking stunning in a dark green dress with gold embroidery on the bodice, the long sleeves, and the hem of the skirt. Kara turned away from the mirror she'd been admiring herself in to see who had come in.

The same happiness that filled my heart upon seeing her beloved face lit up her features.

"Astrid!" Kara exclaimed, before running towards me.

I did the same, and we met halfway, colliding rather brutally with each other. We embraced with something akin to desperation. Gods, how I had missed her! While our personalities couldn't have been more different, Kara and I had always been inseparable growing up. With our mother being taken from us much too soon, we'd heavily relied on each other. Being deprived of her support during this trial hurt me more than anyone realized.

With much reluctance, I finally released my sister, only to hold her by the shoulders as I took in her appearance. Like me, she'd inherited our mother's golden hair. But where my eyes were amber and my skin fairly tan, Kara had sparkling blue eyes and the fairest of skins.

"You look radiant," I said, my voice filled with emotion.

"So do you," Kara replied with a trembling laugh. "I know you said you'd been doing fine. But seeing you so well, glowing almost…"

Kara's voice broke. Her lips quivered, and her eyes misted. My chest constricted with both guilt and love as I drew her back into my arms. I didn't regret going to the ball, but I hated the distress this caused my sister.

Despite her obvious curiosity, Tora mumbled something about fetching some tea and hurried out of the room.

"It's okay, Kara. I am truly fine, I promise," I whispered while gently caressing her hair.

My sister held me a moment longer, her silky, curly hair rubbing softly against my cheek when she nodded.

"Sorry about that," Kara said with a sheepish expression as she let go of me. "I promised not to make a spectacle of myself, and yet here I am slobbering all over you, our Queen no less."

I chuckled and waved a dismissive hand. "My shoulder is always yours to cry on whenever you want. And to you, I'm not the Queen. I'm just your older sister who missed you terribly."

"I missed you, too," Kara said with a sweet smile.

Taking her hand, I led her to the settee next to the privacy screen. She sat by my side, and I held onto her hand—clasped between both of mine—and rested them in my lap.

"How are things at home? How's father?" I asked.

Kara gave me an apologetic look laced with guilt. "Thanks to you, things are almost perfect now. You're the only thing missing. No more collectors are banging down our doors. We have servants again, meat at every meal instead of only once or twice a week. Papa even got Sora back."

I pressed a palm to my chest from shock. "Sora?! Father got Mama's harp back?"

Kara nodded, her eyes misting. "I don't know how much money King Erik gave as your bride token, but it was substantial. Every single one of our debts have been repaid, using less than a third of that amount."

"Dear Gods! That's an insane amount of money!" I exclaimed, flabbergasted.

"That's quite the understatement," Kara said, her face reflecting my disbelief. "Father has immediately set aside a generous dowry for me. He's also made some safe investments. According to him, because they are safe, they will not make a lot of profit, but they will ensure we are comfortable for the rest of our lives, no matter what happens."

I smiled. "That's really good to hear. I went to the ball for that specific reason."

"And you accomplished what you set out to do. I just wish you didn't have to sacrifice yourself for us," Kara said, guilt settling again over her features.

"It was my duty, as the oldest child. However, it may have started as a sacrifice, but now I believe it's turning into the greatest gift from the Gods. Erik is wonderful. He's so kind and generous, always bringing me thoughtful presents, always eager to please me. And yet, it's just his company I enjoy. Aside from the fact that my husband is extremely handsome, he's very charming, witty, and makes me feel like he actually cares about me as a person, as his wife—not just like a tool to break a curse."

Kara narrowed her eyes at me while studying my features. "You sound like you're in love with the King."

I shrugged, my face heating. "I don't know that *in love* is accurate. That feels a little too strong. But I won't deny that I deeply care about him. I can see myself falling madly in love with him. We're still getting to know each other, and…"

"And?" Kara insisted when my voice trailed off.

I shifted uneasily on the settee, wondering just how candid I wanted to be with my sister. We'd never had secrets from each other. Then again, one of us had never been in the grip of a deadly curse. Still, I missed having someone I could openly confide in about this entire ordeal.

"Well, even though Erik is very affectionate, he's clearly keeping his heart from me," I confessed, feeling a little dejected. "I can't even blame him for that. Losing one wife after another has been an endless nightmare. In his stead, I wouldn't want to allow myself to fall in love with someone I might lose again."

"Except he *won't* lose *you*," Kara interjected forcefully while giving me a stern glare.

I smiled and shook my head. "He won't. I'm not going anywhere. Frankly, this whole thing has been more of an inconvenience than an actual challenge. The hardest part isn't resisting temptation, but dealing with the fact that everyone avoids me for fear of getting attached. As much as I like my privacy, I hate being this isolated."

"Temptation? What exactly is the challenge? You've remained vague every time I asked you about it in my letters," Kara said with an adorable pout.

I smiled again and squeezed her hand. "I'm not trying to be secretive. It's just that I genuinely don't know much more than what I've told you. There's a door in the dungeon that must remain sealed. On the first day of every month, I must use this medallion as a key in a special keyhole of the door to activate one of the twelve seals," I explained, showing her the medallion around my neck.

"It's glowing," Kara exclaimed while looking at it warily.

"Yes, and its glow will intensify until the end of the month. Once I use it on the door, it will transfer its energy to it to keep whatever is beyond that door from getting out."

"What *is* beyond that door?" she asked.

I shrugged. "I don't know, and frankly, I don't want to ask."

"Why not?" Kara challenged, taken aback by my response.

58

"Because the whole point of this is to avoid temptation—the temptation of opening that door. What if Erik tells me something that will awaken a burning urge for me to get it or at least see it?"

Kara huffed and waved a dismissive hand. "You are the least nosy person I've ever met."

"Be that as it may, the less I know, the less likely I am to be tempted. The only information I want from Erik as far as this curse is concerned, is what I can and cannot do, and what to look out for. Anything else I don't want to hear about. It's just trouble waiting to happen."

Kara shook her head affectionately at me. "Clearly, you are better suited for this challenge than I am. I would want to know everything and likely get in trouble for it." Even as she spoke those last words, she sobered and gave me a concerned look. "You're really doing fine with this challenge?"

I smiled and nodded. "Yes, Kara. I promise. It has not been difficult so far. What would make it even easier was if you would come visit me at the castle."

My heart broke when she averted her eyes and slightly turned her face away from me. It had been unfair of me to bring it up, knowing it was beyond her power.

"He mourns you, you know?" Kara suddenly said in a pained voice. "Papa thinks it is better we mourn you now so that it will be a little less painful when…"

I clenched my teeth, anger flaring through me. "When nothing!" I snapped. "I have no intention of failing. If he had any backbone, he would be here supporting me, helping me through this rather than assuming the worst."

"He can't because he blames himself," Kara said vehemently. "He said that first, he killed Mother. Now he's killed you. So now he demands that I get married quickly before he kills me, too."

"What? He didn't kill Mother! He didn't kill me!" I argued, baffled. "Mama died in childbirth!"

"From a child *he* put inside her," Kara replied. "And you 'sacrificed' yourself to repay the debts *he* incurred."

"Neither of those tragedies were his fault. It was a complicated pregnancy. It happens. The squall that sunk our ships with all their cargo also wasn't his fault. It was the will of the Gods," I countered.

"*I* know that, but *he* sees it as signs that the Gods are punishing him by taking away the ones he loves," Kara said in a gentle voice.

"Or maybe Mother's death was just a terrible tragedy. And us losing our wealth was merely the Gods laying down the path necessary to drive me to that ball so that I could meet Erik and that, together, we can bring peace to Rathlin by ending that curse."

"I pray you are right, Astrid," she said fervently.

"Of course, I am. I'm always right," I said teasingly.

She snorted and looked at me affectionately. "Do not think too harshly of Father. He loves you. He's heartbroken and berating himself."

"I am hurt, but I understand. By the time the year is up, he will know he wasn't to blame, and this had been the right decision."

"Not one year. Ten and a half months," Kara corrected.

"Indeed," I conceded with a grin. "Now tell me about those suitors Father wants you to marry."

My sister blushed prettily, then told me about the throng of suitors who had come knocking now that our family's wealth had been restored. A part of me hated that many of these young men were only interested in money—or were pressured into striking that match by their family. However, Kara had a good head on her shoulders, and Father wouldn't pressure her into a marriage of convenience. He loved our mother dearly and wished the same for us.

Tora finally returned with tea. I suspected she had deliberately lingered outside to give us some time to speak in private, which I appreciated. We spent the next half hour chatting amiably while Kara tried on new dresses, and Tora adjusted the fit, taking copious notes on the modifications she would make.

"Let's go to Sigrid's bakery," I said with a voracious expression as my sister was finishing putting her original clothes back on. "I can stay for another thirty to forty minutes before I have to head back to the castle. And you know how I can't resist the gooey goodness that are her hot spice and cinnamon buns."

Kara burst out laughing. "You are hopeless! But who am I to challenge the will of the Queen?"

"Good answer," I replied with a grin.

Hooking my arm to hers, we waved goodbye at Tora, then I led my sister out of the private salon. We no sooner exited the room than an all too familiar voice called out to me.

"Lady Astrid! Err... Apologies, your Majesty," Hilda said, with a much too bright smile. "What a coincidence that we should visit Tora on the same day and at the same time."

My heart sank, and I plastered a gracious smile on my face. Of all the rotten coincidences... Then again, I doubted luck had anything to do with this. I'd been here for an hour now. Word of Bluebeard's latest cursed Queen traipsing around town had certainly circulated far and wide. But why would she seek me out? The last time we met, Erik publicly humiliated her.

The way Kara's arm tightened its hold around mine betrayed her tension. Erik soundly dismissing Hilda in my favor had given gossipers much to wag their tongues about. Was she still bitter about it and looking for a fight?

"Lady Hilda," I said politely. "While I had indeed not expected to run into you, it doesn't surprise me. Tora is one of the best modistes of Rathlin. It is therefore normal for ladies of discriminating taste to come see her wares."

Her eyes widened in surprise at the compliment. Did she think I would gloat and rub my 'victory' in her face? Hilda quickly regained her composure and gave me an almost demure smile in acknowledgement.

"Your Majesty is quite right. Tora's creations are exquisite," her once again overly friendly grin making me somewhat uneasy. "It is good to see you looking so well. No wonder everyone in town is in such high spirits. It has been too long since a queen mingled with us. But then, I didn't realize the King's bride could leave the castle."

I barely repressed the urge to roll my eyes at such an obvious attempt at fishing for information.

"As you can see, I can," I replied matter-of-factly.

"Indeed. But now that I have you here, would it be too bold to ask what exactly the challenge is?"

The greed with which she asked further increased my unease. However, the deafening silence that followed her words made me look around the room. The unusually high number of patrons finally sank in, as well as the fact that every whispered conversation had stopped as they all eagerly awaited my answer.

I groaned inwardly. "The challenge is to resist temptation," I said nonchalantly, before turning to look at my sister. "But one temptation I do not have to resist is a spicy cinnamon roll from Sigrid's. If you would excuse us."

Pulling Kara after me, I started walking away.

"Your Majesty! You can't leave like this!" Hilda exclaimed, her face displaying the same disappointment—not to say disbelief—as everyone else in the room. "Won't you sate our curiosity as to what has caused Rathlin to lose so many of its daughters?"

My spine stiffened, and I clenched my teeth at such shameless emotional blackmail. I stopped and turned to look at her, this time with far less warmth.

"If King Erik wanted to give details about the challenge is, he would have done so years ago. It is not my place to make such a decision on his behalf. I have told you what I could. For anything else, you will have to ask the King himself. Now, if you'll excuse me, my sister and I have other plans."

With that, I led my sister out of the boutique.

CHAPTER 7

ERIK

I headed up to the gallery with heavy steps. After my official visit to the city of Leif, I just wanted to spend some time relaxing with my wife. But duty—always duty—came first. In this instance, as she'd undoubtedly still be in her greenhouse, the timing was perfect. Astrid had been distraught enough the first time she'd stumbled on the portraits of my previous wives. She didn't need to know I was meeting with the artist who would draw hers.

My chest constricted when I pushed open the large doors into the gallery. Twenty-seven far too familiar faces stared back at me with accusatory or betrayed eyes. As much as I tried to ease my conscience by reminding myself that they had volunteered for this, my heart still ached that they had all died too soon. Some of them, I'd genuinely cared about. They deserved so much better. I'd failed them. Even though it had been their challenge to overcome, surely there was something more that I could have done.

An irrational anger—if not hatred—swelled within me at the sight of Ogden, already busy sketching Astrid's portrait. Sitting on a stool, his frail silhouette hunched over his sketchbook, he was moving his chalk with swift and confident movements. His graying, long black hair dangled in a curtain on each side of his narrow face. I had no reason to resent him. The older male was merely exercising his profession.

As the main artist retained by nobles for their portraits, he knew pretty much everyone, including my Astrid. Therefore, although I had provided Ogden with a miniature portrait of my wife, he appeared to be working from memory.

He lifted his head to level his pale green eyes on me upon hearing my approach.

"Your Majesty," he said, jumping off his stool to bow in greeting.

Although he smiled, it was devoid of his usual cheerful disposition and held instead the appropriate solemn edge under the circumstances.

"Master Ogden," I replied in a similar tone. "I see you're already at work."

"I am, your Highness. Here are a few sketches for you to review."

I perused the sheets he handed me, each sketch—as exquisite as the other—captured a unique trait of my wife's personality. Although the first one, showing her in a regal pose, would have been more fitting, I kept returning to the one where she had a wistful expression, a discreet smile stretching her lips at whatever pleasant thoughts flitted through her mind. I'd caught her looking at me that way once or twice. My gut told me those were moments where she felt happy being with me, despite our circumstances. At least, I *wanted* to believe I gave her moments of happiness.

"This one," I said, finally settling on the wistful portrait.

"An excellent choice, my King," Ogden said with approval. "I will start working on it at once."

"Before you go, I would like to order a second portrait of my wife, life size," I blurted. "I want you to paint Astrid playing the harp in the music room. You may ask her to pose for that one, should you require it. But not a word about the first," I warned sternly.

"Of course not, your Highness," Ogden replied swiftly, sounding a little offended. "I am well-aware of the need for discretion in this matter. In all the years I've served you, I have always held myself to the highest standards of professionalism."

"Of course, you have," I conceded, slightly ashamed. "I hadn't meant to imply otherwise. But when it comes to Astrid, I tend to be a little overprotective."

My own words, this admission of deeper feelings for my wife, stunned me. Beyond the fact that I was never one to admit a weakness or vulnerability, the realization of how much I cared for Astrid terrified me.

Mollified, Ogden softened, a sliver of commiseration entering his expression. "Yes, I can see why you would be. I watched Lady Astrid grow into a delightful young woman, always so caring and devoted to others. She is the perfect queen for our realm."

I nodded and replied with a non-committal grunt, annoyed with myself.

"I do not believe that posing the Queen will be necessary for the harp painting," Ogden continued, when an awkward silence settled between us. "It will be a delightful surprise for her once it's completed. However, with your permission, I would like to go have a look at the music room to refresh my memory as to its layout."

"By all means, do. I believe you know the way?" I asked, eager to be rid of him.

"That's correct, I do. Good day to you, your Majesty."

"And to you as well, Ogden."

I watched him leave, heaving a sigh when the door closed behind him. The weight of my deceased wives' stares drew my attention back to the wall. Twenty-seven. A part of me wondered why I kept doing this to myself. I didn't want to add a twenty-eighth portrait there. And yet I owed them as much.

In truth, I wasn't trying to punish myself with this. But they deserved to be immortalized. It also served as a visual reminder of the sacrifices we were making to keep our world safe from a monster. I survived this many battles, I would survive another.

"Really, King Erik? Will you survive the demise of your new little wife?"

My spine stiffened at the sound of the hated voice resonating in my head. I ignored it, refusing to give the fiend any additional power over me.

A malicious chuckle echoed in my mind.

"Tsk, tsk. It is rude not to answer a question. But I don't need you to. You've never ordered a special portrait before. Has the golden maiden captured Bluebeard's dark and shriveled little heart?"

Clenching my teeth, I closed my eyes and took a deep breath to rein in my emotions.

"Once you've killed her—and you will—may I hope you will also add that life-size masterpiece to my trophy room alongside the others who miserably failed? Tick tock, Erik. Enjoy your little wife while you can. Your time is running out."

"SILENCE, YOU WRETCHED VERMIN!" I shouted, anger boiling within my veins.

Even as more evil laughter filled my mind, the gallery's door burst open on a worried Tormund.

"Your Majesty? Is everything all right?"

His eyes flicked around the room, looking for whoever might have stirred my ire. Finding me alone, his face paled with under-standing. Although no one knew exactly what abomination lurked in the dungeon, Tormund had figured out a few things over the years. Not for the first time, I considered revealing everything to him. However, that would require me to also expose part of my true nature. I didn't know that he was ready for it.

Straightening my shoulders and forcing a neutral expression on my face, I shook my head at Tormund and gave him a stiff smile.

"Yes, everything is fine. You were looking for me?" I asked.

By the way he hesitated, he wanted to insist and pry further. My stern stare made it abundantly clear he was to drop it. Tormund swallowed hard and complied.

"Yes, your Majesty. I thought you should know that Queen Astrid is not at the castle right now," he replied.

I blinked, confused as to why he felt the need to tell me something I already knew, or at least suspected. "Why, yes. She spends her days at her greenhouse."

"Not today. After your departure for Leif this morning, the Queen received a message from her sister, inviting her to join her at a fitting at the modiste in Revna," he explained. "She's been gone two hours now."

"WHAT?! Why in the world would you let her go to the city?" I shouted, fear, anger, and disbelief battling for dominance within me.

"She had already discussed the matter with you, your Majesty," Tormund replied in a defensive tone. "I reminded her she needed to be back within four hours or—"

"THREE! THREE HOURS, YOU FOOL!" I exclaimed, fighting the urge to strangle him. "You should have told her to be back within three hours. What if her carriage gets damaged on the way back? What if a storm or other elements beyond her control impedes her ability to return? You must account for potential delays. If she fails to be back in time, all of this will have been for naught!"

"I'm sorry, your Majesty—"

"Spare me your apologies!" I snapped shoving past him.

As I ran to the door, the evil laughter resonated once more in my mind.

"Tick tock, tick tock, little king."

I stormed out of the castle, Tormund on my heels, and shouted for Thunder to be brought to me at once, even as I raced towards the stables. The stable boy started putting the saddle on my horse, moving far slower than I needed him to. Losing patience, I pushed him aside and finished the task myself while my guards frantically saddled their own mounts. As soon as I finished, I hopped onto Thunder's back and began racing towards the city.

I ignored my guards calling out my name, along with the nagging voice that kept taunting me about Astrid's imminent demise. Thankfully, it dimmed as the distance from the castle increased. My gaze kept flicking to my ring to make sure its gem remained white. It was linked to the necklace. If it ever turned pink, I would know either Astrid had opened the Sealed Door, or the necklace's defense mechanism had triggered because of her excessively long absence from the castle.

I rode Thunder hard, grateful for the mostly clear sky above, and the relatively scarce traffic on the main road. Each time I saw a carriage coming from the opposite direction, my heart leapt for a second, hoping it would be Astrid on her way back to the castle. Every time they turned out not to be my wife, my anger went up another notch.

Yes, I had discussed the possibility of Astrid going to town. Yes, I had also stated that she couldn't be gone for more than four hours. However, beyond the fact that I had always assumed that I would be with her the day she did, this time frame wasn't a perfect mathematical equation with a guaranteed result. The grace period outside of the castle grounds could be longer or shorter. Only once the medallion turned pink or red would we know for certain that time was up. She should have erred on the side of caution.

Considering how her father kept Kara from visiting, I understood that she had rushed to see her sister the minute the message came in. Who knew when another opportunity would arise? But it felt incredibly irresponsible for her to still be in town after all this time. Not only did her life depend on her being back in time, but so did the safety of the entire realm. However trapped she felt inside the castle was irrelevant. She committed to taking on this challenge, with all that it entailed.

After what felt like an eternity, I finally closed in on the city. I slowed down the punishing pace I'd imposed on Thunder, feeling guilty for pushing him so hard. This gave my guards a chance to catch up to me, allowing us to enter the city with a semblance of decorum. I didn't even want to imagine how disheveled I might look from the wind that had blown through my hair during this mad race to Revna.

My heart sank as I approached Tora's boutique and didn't see the royal carriage outside, or any signs of her guards. Barely waiting for Thunder to come to a halt, I hopped off his back and marched to the entrance, to my guards' dismay.

"Your Majesty," Tora exclaimed, discarding the dress she was holding onto the counter before rushing towards me.

"Where's the Queen?" I demanded, not waiting for her to finish bowing.

She looked confused. "Queen Astrid? She left, your Majesty. She and her sister left over thirty minutes ago."

My chest constricted with mounting fear. Where had she gone to? She hadn't left the city, or we would have crossed paths. The dreadful thought that she might go visit her father crossed my mind. If she'd left the modiste thirty minutes ago, she would never reach her father's estate and make it back to the castle in time.

She wouldn't be so foolish.

"Where did they go?" I demanded, my voice so sharp Tora recoiled, fear settling over her features.

I hadn't meant to frighten the sweet older woman, but I needed to find Astrid.

"She... The Queen mentioned Sigrid's cinnamon buns. So—"

I didn't wait for the rest of her sentence and stormed out of her boutique. Jumping back onto my horse, I raced down the two blocks to Sigrid's bakery. I almost wept with relief at the sight of the royal carriage. But anger quickly replaced the sentiment when I noticed my wife standing outside of the bakery, having an animated conversation with her sister. Was she so clueless, or did she not care that time was ticking? In my mind, I could hear my tormentor's hated voice saying 'tick tock, tick tock', further fueling my anger at Astrid.

I couldn't tell whether the sound of Thunder's hooves quickly approaching, or the sudden gasps and surprised expressions of the nearby passersby alerted her to my presence, but Astrid suddenly turned to look curiously in my direction. She recoiled, shock giving way to wariness as I approached, allowing her to see the look on my face.

"Erik?" Astrid said questioningly when I jumped off my horse and marched towards her.

"We're leaving, at once," I said through my teeth.

"But—"

"NOW, Astrid! Get in the carriage," I ordered in a tone that brooked no argument.

She paled, confusion and fear etching over her beautiful features. I hated that I was the one stirring such emotions in her, but I was too angry to think straight. By the way she looked at the silent crowd staring at us, before giving a quick hug to her sister, I realized just how humiliating this must be for her. I once again kicked myself for my visceral reaction. Publicly embarrassing her had never been my intention. And yet, I couldn't let such concerns deter me from my current course of action. I was trying to save her from herself, from the curse, while also protecting the realm.

After giving Kara a stiff nod, I followed Astrid towards our carriage. This had not been the first impression I had wanted to give my wife's sibling. The worried—not to say horrified—look she gave me hinted she thought me a monster, or likely an abusive husband. That, too, made me angrier.

One of Astrid's guards hurried to open the carriage door for us. A single look at my face let him know both he and his unit were going to have to answer to me for not telling her to leave sooner. Making eye contact with one of my own guards, I gestured with my chin at Thunder. He nodded in response, understanding that he was to bring him back to the castle while I used the carriage with my wife.

Just as Astrid was getting inside our transportation, Lord Arne's aggravating voice called out my name.

"Your Majesty! King Erik! How fortuitous to see you here!" the portly man exclaimed while running towards me with impressive speed for his size.

"Whatever it is, it will have to wait. I'm in a hurry," I said sternly.

"Oh, but I just need a minute," he argued in an overly enthusiastic voice. "It will be swift."

Annoyed beyond words, I turned to face the man dead on, locked eyes with him, and dropped the pitch of my voice.

"You will *not* take any more of my time. Forget you saw me, and leave," I said in a dangerously calm tone.

His eyes increasingly glazed over with each of my words as the subtle vibration in my voice reinforced the compulsion. Looking dazed, Lord Arne turned on his heel and walked away.

Astrid, who had settled inside the carriage, was observing me with a baffled expression, her brow creasing even more as she stretched her neck to look at Arne walking away. I cursed the man inwardly for making me further expose myself.

As I climbed inside, Astrid gathered her skirt around her legs then clasped her hands in her lap. I sat in the seat across from her, my teeth still clenched in anger as I stared at my wife. As soon as the guard closed the door, I struck the wall with my fist twice to let the driver know to get going. Seconds later, the carriage started moving.

Astrid swallowed hard while I continued to glare at her.

"What's going on, Erik? Why are you so upset?" she asked in a trembling voice.

I tilted my head to the side as I looked at her in disbelief. "Why? Why am I upset?"

"We already discussed me coming to town to see my sister," she argued, visibly still confused. "You were fine with it."

"I was fine with it assuming you'd do so within reason. How long have you been gone, Astrid?" I snarled.

She blinked, then gaped at me with understanding before taking on an outraged expression. "I've been gone less than three hours. When you arrived, it was two hours and forty-five minutes. I was going to leave within the next ten minutes. You said to be back within four hours. I would have been back at the castle with twenty-five minutes to spare!"

"Would you have, Astrid? Are you certain?" I retorted with a challenge in my voice. "What if the carriage hit a pothole on the way back and it either got stuck or one wheel was damaged? What if a horse got a sharp stone in its hoof that forced the driver to stop and remove it so it wouldn't limp all the way home? What if some farmer decided now was the time to have his herd crossing the main road, blocking the path for half an hour? Do I need to give you more what ifs?"

Astrid blanched a little more with each of my words.

"I understand you feel trapped inside the castle, and that you miss your sister. But I need you to be more responsible. Too many lives depend on you, not to mention your own. Four hours is merely an approximation. It could be twenty to thirty minutes less because of such a great distance between the necklace and the castle. You cannot play with this, Astrid. I need to know that I can trust you to account for such things."

She hugged herself and bowed her head with an air of guilt and shame. In that instant, I felt like a monster. She'd looked so happy while conversing with her sister. Knowing that I had ruined what had likely been one of the nicer days Astrid had enjoyed since our marriage twisted my insides. And yet, I couldn't back down from this. She needed to understand the seriousness of her situation.

But how can she when it has been so easy for her so far?

And it had indeed been disturbingly easy for her, not that I would complain about it. All of my previous wives had begun hearing voices within the first month, even Ariana who had outlasted all the others. Aside from the temporary pain from activating the first seal a couple of weeks ago, Astrid hadn't shown any signs just yet of being subjected to temptation. While it gave me hope that this indicated she might finally be the one to break the curse, it also gave her a deceptive sense of confidence that this was no true challenge. But it *would* get impossibly challenging. As much as I didn't want to needlessly scare her, I couldn't let her grow nonchalant about this.

"I'm sorry, Erik," Astrid said in a contrite voice. "You're right, I should have accounted for the possibility of unexpected mishaps. You shouldn't have had to come fetch me. I will try to do better in the future."

I grunted in a non-committal fashion, not really knowing what to say, yet hating the tension between us. We remained quiet for the duration of the trip back home, each of us lost in our own thoughts. On more than one occasion, I almost said something to strike a casual conversation. But every time, either words failed me, or the topic felt stupid and forced.

It didn't help that I kept glancing in turn at Astrid's necklace and at my ring to make sure they remained white. Every time she caught me doing so, her guilt and shame resurfaced, further making me feel horrible about this mess.

Thankfully, no unexpected incident delayed our return. Only once we passed the castle's grounds' front gates did the tension that had been holding my spine in a vise finally relent.

Tormund's relief when we exited the carriage was palpable. I nodded at him in response to his welcome. I would have to apologize to him later. Like Astrid, he had not deserved for me to address him so harshly.

Heaving a sigh, I entered the castle, my chest tightening as my wife headed straight for her boudoir. At least, the wretched voice wasn't taunting me, no doubt because there was nothing to brag about as the medallion had returned to the castle in time.

I headed into my study and retrieved a flat box, rehearsing in a million different ways how I was going to make amends with my woman. After going back and forth much too long, I squared my shoulders and decided to just go for it. Once in front of the door of Astrid's boudoir, my nerves nearly got the best of me. What a pathetic king and husband I made. I could stare down any head of state, lead armies when needed, and even defeat a kraken. Yet, here I was, ready to cower in retreat instead of facing my wife.

Raising my hand, I rapped my knuckles against the door. Almost immediately, Astrid's muffled voice bid me come in. I took in a deep, fortifying breath and proceeded.

I found my wife sitting at the secretary, a quill in hand as she was likely writing a letter to her sister to explain her abrupt departure. Her lips parted in surprise at seeing me. She probably expected it to be a servant asking what she wanted for dinner.

"Erik... Please, come in," she said.

The odd mix of hope and wariness in her voice and expression tugged at my heart. At least, it seemed to indicate that she, too, wanted to put this mess behind us.

"I... uh... I have something for you," I said, flinching

inwardly as my feet moved me towards her as if with a will of their own. That was *not* how I had wanted to handle the situation.

"Oh?" Astrid said, her eyes lighting up with curiosity as she reached for the ornate wooden box I was extending to her.

My wife moved the piece of parchment paper she'd been writing on and carefully placed the box on top of the desk in front of her. Her fingers gently caressed the swirling pattern carved into the polished wood. She released the clasp keeping the box closed and lifted the lid.

Her eyes widened first in surprise and then in admiration at the exquisite jewelry set within comprising a necklace, earrings, and bracelet, each with a large orange sapphire.

"Thank you, Erik. It's beautiful," Astrid said in a hushed voice, an uneasy expression on her face.

"I immediately thought of you when I saw it. The stones perfectly matched the amber color of your eyes," I said, feeling awkward.

"Yeah, they do," she said with a somewhat stiff smile.

I cleared my throat and scratched my beard. "I... I also wanted to apologize for being so harsh earlier. When I found out you'd gone to Revna, I panicked and handled it poorly."

She gave me a timid smile. "It's all right. You had valid reasons to be upset."

"I did," I concurred. "But in retrospect, I have to admit that my anger was equally aimed at you as it was at myself."

Astrid's brows shot up, and she looked at me with confusion. "At yourself? Why?"

"Because I should have explained the situation to you better," I said, running a frustrated hand through my hair. "I've been living with this nightmare for so long that I forget that all of this is still new to you. You do not know everything that I do. Making sure that you have all the information necessary to make enlightened decisions is on me. I failed you in that. Yes, I wish you had accounted for contingencies, but you had no reason to think you might have less than four hours. And that is *my* fault. You said you will do better. However, I must do the same as well instead of just assuming you know what's in my head."

A powerful emotion crossed Astrid's beautiful face, and her golden eyes misted. The quivering smile she gave me, filled with gratitude, made me realize she'd felt like I'd treated her unfairly in my anger—which I had.

I extended a hand towards her. She took it willingly and rose to her feet. I pulled her into my embrace and gently caressed her cheek.

"I'm sorry for ruining the pleasant day you had with your sister. It shames me to admit that fear largely fueled my anger. The thought that you might not make it back to the castle..."

I shook my head, my voice trailing off as I forced myself to cast out the horrible images flashing through my mind.

"And I'm sorry that my carelessness put you through this ordeal. You were right in everything you said in the carriage. Yes, it upset me, but I should have thought about it. I was just so excited about seeing Kara again that I threw all caution to the wind. I *will* do better in the future. And that will be even easier if you *indeed* share with me clear guidance about what I can and cannot do, as well as what to watch out for."

"I promise, I will," I said with fervor.

Eyes locked with Astrid, I leaned down, my lips stopping a hair's breadth from hers. She smiled and lifted her face, closing the short distance between us to kiss me. My arms tightened around my wife, my heart filling with affection and relief. I didn't want us to fight.

When we broke the kiss, Astrid caressed my cheek before casting an amused glance at the jewelry box.

"It is a lovely present, but you don't have to buy my forgiveness with jewelry," she said teasingly.

I snorted. "I didn't buy it for that. While in Leif this morning,

I saw it in a store and immediately knew I had to get it for you. In case you haven't noticed yet, I love spoiling you. As much as I want your help getting rid of this curse, I genuinely care about you, Astrid. I sincerely do."

She melted against me and once more gazed upon me with that air of wonder filled with affection that always did a number on me.

"Good, because I deeply care about you, too, Erik."

I smiled and reclaimed her lips.

CHAPTER 8
ASTRID

Already four months had gone by since the fateful day I had disobeyed my father and presented myself as an aspiring bride to King Erik Thorsen. Four months of facing a challenge that didn't feel like one, except on the first day of every month. Activating the seals was not only draining but also increasingly painful, like a part of me was being torn out. Erik assured me it caused me no harm. Indeed, aside from the short-lived pain during the activation, and the bone deep weariness in the hours that followed, I seemed to suffer no aftermath.

It confused me that it was so easy when twenty-seven women before me had failed so miserably. Ariana, Erik's last wife, had lasted four months longer than everyone else for a total of six months. Was the effectiveness of the curse waning? Either way, I wouldn't complain.

My real challenge was loneliness. Father still wouldn't let Kara come visit me, and after the previous incident in town, I limited my number of trips there and kept them short to avoid the medallion turning red on me. This curse wouldn't defeat me simply because I itched to wander away from the castle. There would be plenty of time for that once this year was up.

At least, I had Erik.

He was the perfect husband. Despite his many responsibilities, he always made time for me. He was kind, tender and attentive. Erik sought every opportunity to spoil me. While I wasn't materialistic, his little presents touched me deeply because they were personal. Knowing my passion for botany and books, Erik had brought back the best gift from his last diplomatic travel: a full collection of illuminated books on the caring for and growing of exotic plants in a northern climate. Whenever possible, he would also bring me rare seeds, and the finest gold and silk threads for my embroidery.

Though he sought my advice or opinion on some matters, Erik didn't involve me in the affairs of the state. However, as his queen, I should carry part of the royal burden, mainly through social events and diplomatic visits. I should also nurture harmonious relations between the people and the crown, counsel Erik, and support him in whatever capacity he required. I truly looked forward to that. The castle was far too beautiful to be reduced to no more than a mausoleum.

But with the sword of Damocles hanging over my head, I would remain in the shadows until the trial was over. There was no point in forming friendships with allies and other counterparts if I was to be replaced weeks later by another.

I believed this was the reason Erik was so generous, giving me everything but himself. Granted, he seemed to genuinely enjoy my company and, far from waning, his insatiable hunger for me had increased over time. However, he kept his heart tightly closed off to me. I understood why he didn't allow himself such vulnerability with this curse, but that didn't stop me from wanting a real bond with my husband. I cared deeply for Erik. In fact, I was falling in love with him, and I wanted the same from him.

The mid-summer afternoon sun shone through the large windows of Erik's study. Sitting behind his massive desk, he was reviewing the amendments to some trade agreements with a neighboring state. I sat by the fireplace across from him, doing the gold work on a cloak I was embroidering for him.

"Astrid."

"Yes, Erik?" I asked, glancing at him. To my surprise, he was still hard at work.

Raising his head from the documents he was poring over, he gave me a confused look. "Excuse me?"

"Err... You called my name. Did you need something?"

Erik reclined in his chair with a frown. "No. I did not call your name, Astrid."

I stared at him for a moment, just as confused as he seemed. "Strange. I could have sworn someone called me. Sorry for disturbing you," I said with an apologetic smile.

I resumed my embroidery, but his stillness drew my attention back to him. Erik continued to observe me, as if seeking some kind of answer. Unnerved by his intense gaze, I squirmed on the couch.

"Was it my voice you thought you heard?" he asked.

"There are only the two of us here, Erik," I said, gesturing at the room.

He waved an impatient hand. "I'm well aware of that, but that wasn't my question. The voice you heard, did it sound like me?"

His strange behavior baffled me. "Well... Hmm... I didn't really pay attention," I said with a shrug. "I heard a voice calling me and automatically assumed it was yours since we're alone here. But no, I can't swear it sounded like you... not that it matters, since I clearly imagined it."

The expression on Erik's face could only be interpreted as sad. He rubbed his face with both hands before leaning back over the documents on his desk. There was something he wasn't telling me.

"What's wrong? Why are you so troubled? It was just a mistake."

His smile was meant to be reassuring, but he remained too tense for it to be believable. "There's nothing wrong, my darling. Forgive me. These trade agreements are driving me to distraction. I should be done shortly. Would you care to join me on a ride afterward?"

"I would love that," I said with genuine enthusiasm.

He nodded, apparently pleased with my answer and returned his attention to the documents before him. I resumed my embroidery work, not realizing that this moment had marked the beginning of a rift between us that would deepen over the following weeks.

While still being his charming self, Erik became distant. He spent time with me as much as he always had, but he wasn't as affectionate anymore. He no longer randomly pulled me in his lap to nuzzle my nape while telling me of his day. There were no more impromptu visits to my boudoir just because he missed me. His smiles were less frequent, and no longer reached his eyes. He was still as passionate with me at night, but with an urgency that bordered on desperation.

It reminded me too much of that first time he had left me alone in the castle for two weeks. When I asked him what was wrong, he kept saying everything was fine. We both knew it wasn't true. However, I couldn't call him out on it without accusing him of being a liar. It was breaking my heart, but I didn't know what to do.

I started hearing voices calling my name or saying random, nonsensical things, more and more frequently. At first, it was every other day. Then it was once a day. Now, I stopped counting the occurrences. I wondered if I was going insane from lack of human contact other than with Erik. Maybe I had become so starved for social interaction that I had invented an imaginary companion. After all, the voices called to me more frequently when I was alone. I wanted to talk to Erik about it, but there was already too much distance between us. I didn't want him thinking me crazy, too.

Lying on my back, I turned to look at the sleeping form of my husband. We had made love tonight. As always, Erik had been a generous and passionate lover. But after we both found our release, he turned on his side, his back to me and went to sleep. Erik used to hold me close after our lovemaking. He would wrap himself around me and wouldn't let go, as if he feared I would go away or disappear. But now…

I looked down at the medallion resting on my chest. It glowed brightly. August was only two days away. With it, the fifth seal would be activated. I couldn't wait for that to be over. Stealing a glance at Erik's back, I fought the urge to cuddle against him. As much as it hurt, I wouldn't beg for his affection. The hour was late, and I needed to sleep. Turning on my side, with my back to his, I closed my eyes.

The ever-elusive sleep must have finally claimed me because the next thing I knew, I was standing in the underbrush leading to my greenhouse. I could hear a faint voice in the distance. Curious as to who would intrude there, I followed the path. But instead of leading to my greenhouse, the path ended at the top of a cliff overlooking a small dock. A battered ship had crashed into it and was taking on water. The voice emanated from within. It was strange that I could hear it from such a distance. Then again, this was a dream...

I opened the gate of the protective railing and climbed the narrow stairs down to the docks. The voice was now stronger, desperately calling for help. It sounded somewhat familiar.

"Hang on, I'm coming!" I shouted.

"Please! Hurry! I don't want to die," a frightened feminine voice replied.

Thankfully, I had no problem getting on the deck of the ship, which was surprisingly flush with the dock, and I raced to the door whence the voice emanated. I looked for a handle, but I couldn't find one. I pushed against the door with all my weight, but it didn't move an inch.

"The door is stuck!" I yelled, still pushing against it. "Is there something blocking it on your side?"

"It's not stuck. It's locked," the voice said. "Please, unlock it. I'm drowning!"

"But how? I don't have the key. There isn't even a keyhole!"

"Yes, there is. Look up, you will see the keyhole," the voice said. "And you have the key around your neck."

Exactly like she said, there was a discreet keyhole in the center of the door. Around my neck, a golden key dangled at the end of a delicate gold chain. I took the key in my hand, frowning. Where did I get that key? Before I had a chance to further analyze my sudden uneasiness, the woman started pounding frantically on the door, begging me to save her. Without thinking, I shoved the key into the hole and turned it left. Or rather, I tried to...

The key resisted all my efforts, and I feared it would break if I insisted. "It doesn't work! The key won't turn!"

"You're turning it the wrong way," the voice said with urgency. "Turn it right. Do it now!"

I froze at her words. A terrible sense of dread washed over me. Something was very wrong here. I couldn't turn the key to the right. Bad things would happen. Erik's words echoed in my head...

"...turn it counterclockwise. Remember, always to the left. Turning it clockwise means death."

"No... I can't. Erik said never to the right."

"This isn't about Erik. Erik is wrong. I'm going to die if you don't help me right away. Turn the key right now. I beg you!"

The slapping sound of footsteps resonated behind me. "Astrid!"

Looking over my shoulder, I saw Erik come to a running stop on the dock. He was barefoot, wearing nothing but his sleeping tunic. His face was drained of color, and he looked terrified.

"Erik! We need your help. The ship is sinking, and the door is locked. We must—"

With his palms raised in a calming gesture, he cautiously approached me.

"Astrid, please... Please take the medallion out of the socket and step away from the door. Please..." he said, his voice quivering with fear.

My anxiety level soared. Why was my fearless Erik so scared? And what did he mean by the medallion? I wasn't using the medallion. It was a golden key. Turning back to the door, I observed the key and suddenly noticed the strange glow around the keyhole. I squinted, and as if a veil was lifted, the battered ship door turned into the Sealed Door, and the golden key into the nautilus.

With a horrified shout, I pulled the medallion out of the socket and hastily backed away. Erik's arms closed around me, and he further dragged me from the door. I clung to him with the energy of despair, my entire body shaking violently. His hand fisting my hair, Erik held me in a crushing embrace. I could feel him trembling against me, the warmth of his labored breath fanning on my neck.

The voice stopped its pleading and suddenly broke into an evil chuckle. "So close... Until next time, Queen Astrid."

"Ignore her, my darling," Erik whispered in my ear. He lifted me in his arms and carried me out of the dungeon.

M y mind kept replaying what had happened. I was finally starting to grasp what Erik had meant that first night when he said the challenge was to resist temptation, although this qualified more as deception. For the first four months, this had been a breeze. The last month had been another story. But contrary to what I had believed, it wasn't madness from extended isolation that plagued me. The voices had been real, insidious. They... no, she had slowly infiltrated my subconscious, and at my most vulnerable moment, lured me with her siren's call to my doom.

Understanding suddenly dawned on me. My gaze flew to Erik, who stood quietly by our bedroom fireplace, staring at me. As I put the pieces together, they fit too perfectly for this to be a mere coincidence.

"What are you, Erik?"

He stilled and narrowed his eyes at me. "I'm your husband."

"Yes. And you're also not human, are you?"

His face closed off, showing no emotion. "Of course, I'm human," he said with a clipped tone. "What else would I be? You've seen my parents, and my mother gave birth to me right here in the castle assisted by the midwife."

"The first time I heard the voice, it was in your study, a month ago." I stood from my seat on the couch in front of the fireplace and paced the room. "You suspected then what was happening. Today, you heard the taunting words she said to me. No one can stay in the castle at night, for fear of their safety, but you can. You fear they will succumb to her lure... to her siren's song, but you don't. And your own voice is often quite... hypnotic. I remember how you sent Lord Arne away with a single sentence when he normally is otherwise impossible to sway."

Erik clenched his jaw at that last comment. I had hit a nerve.

"Your blue hair and silver eyes aren't normal colors for

humans. Having your father or grandfather on a ship guaranteed smooth sailing and safe passage from sea monsters. Hence you've all been called the Sea Kings."

He crossed his arms over his chest and leaned against the mantle of the fireplace. "So what do you think I am, dearest wife?"

I walked over to my jewelry box and pulled out the locket I had found months ago in the greenhouse. Returning to Erik, I extended a closed hand to him. He hesitated for a moment but then presented his open palm. I placed the locket in it.

"I think you're the same as whatever is locked behind that door," I said, matter-of-factly.

Erik blanched when he saw what I had given him. His hands shook when he opened the locket and looked at the portraits staring back at him.

"Where did you find this?" he whispered.

"In the greenhouse..."

Fisting his hand around the locket, he brushed past me and walked to the large window overlooking the courtyard. He pulled the curtains open and stared at the golden outline of the rising sun on the horizon.

"She has your hair and your eyes. He looks just like your father. I'm assuming this is your grandfather, King Harald. She must be the foreign wife we all heard of, but who could not reign by his side, because of her duties in her own kingdom. She looks exactly like the crowned mermaid on the fountain in the abandoned section of the garden."

Erik's shoulders drooped. With a sigh, he turned back to face me, a look of defeat on his face. He gestured to the couch I previously sat on. "Sit down, Astrid."

I complied, folding my robe around me.

"As is taught in history classes, eighty years ago, people deemed conquering the unclaimed Rathlin Islands impossible. Between the kraken and the frequent storms, it was too hazardous. A bold captain decided to challenge that notion. The islands were not only fertile lands, but they were right at the heart of the main merchant trade routes. Whoever controlled them would become rich and powerful. So he set out to defeat the kraken, and like all the others before him, his ship was destroyed."

Erik looked at the portraits in the locket and ran his thumb over the woman's face.

"What history lessons do not say is that Queen Alinor, ruler of the merfolk Kingdom of Llys, fancied the foolish human. He was clinging for dear life on the wreckage of his ship amidst troubled waters. She ordered her Sea Witch to recall the kraken and calm the elements. The Queen and the captain became lovers and eventually married. But Harald was human and couldn't live under the sea."

His wary eyes locked with mine upon those last words, no doubt to gauge my reaction. I nodded and gave him an encouraging—though somewhat strained—smile. He swallowed hard, but some of the tension seemed to drain from his shoulders.

"He became the King of Rathlin Islands so that they could remain close to each other. They had two children. Harald brought their firstborn, my father Brandt, to live among the humans and be his heir to the throne of Rathlin. Their daughter, my Aunt Eira, would rule the Llysians after Queen Alinor. My grandfather remained faithful to his wife and visited her often."

Erik took one last glance at the portraits before closing the locket. He walked over to my vanity near the dresser and placed the locket back in my jewelry box. I shifted restlessly on the couch, knowing he was buying himself some time before delving into the events that had caused this harmonious arrangement to end in the curse that tormented him and threatened my life.

"My father was seventeen when Queen Alinor died. King Harald took him to the funeral so he could pay his final respects to his mother and to bear witness to the crowning of his sister, my Aunt Eira. That's when my father met a young Sea Witch apprentice named Alba. They became lovers, and that liaison lasted twelve years. It ended when the King died, and my father made a politically beneficial marriage to my mother. When he went to end things with Alba, she thought he was coming to ask for her hand. She was devastated, especially because she had just found out she was pregnant."

I knew exactly where this was headed. The curse killed the wives of the ruling king. Of course it would be the revenge of a woman scorned. Erik came to sit next to me, eyeing me warily.

"So you have an older brother, or sister?" I asked softly.

"A sister," Erik said, folding his hands in his lap. "The separation wasn't friendly. A month later, my parents were married and a year after that, I was born. Father took me to Llys to be presented to Queen Eira. She had promoted Alba to Royal Sea Witch. In a gesture of goodwill, Alba told my father she had forgiven him and offered him a jeweled psyche mirror as a present to my mother."

"Please tell me your father didn't give a present to his wife from a scorned former lover?"

"Foolishly naïve, wasn't it?" Erik said, shaking his head. "He did. And for years, all seemed well except that my mother went through one miscarriage or stillbirth after another. With each one, my mother became more and more reclusive, spending an unhealthy amount of time in front of her psyche. That's when they realized something was off with it. I was fifteen when they confronted Alba for her spiteful crime. Queen Eira had her executed, and they sealed off the psyche in the dungeon. They couldn't destroy it without killing my mother. She had too strongly bonded with it. In the end, even that didn't save her."

I put a comforting hand over his. He wrapped his fingers around mine and gave them a gentle squeeze. His expression seemed grateful. I realized he had feared rejection because of his lineage. Part of me had suspected from the moment I had seen the locket so many months ago. But Erik was right. While he had merfolk blood, he was human in all the ways that mattered. He also was my husband; the man I loved.

"So what happened?" I asked. "Did the psyche continue to affect your mother?"

"Not exactly. It could no longer influence her, but she'd grown addicted to it. Mother was going mad from not having access to that wretched mirror. Father took her away from the kingdom for a while to help her recover. A few hours after they left the shore, the kraken attacked and sunk their ship. My half-sister, Traxia, is also a Sea Witch."

I felt myself blanch at the name. Traxia... Suddenly, that strange dream I had when Erik had left for a fortnight came back to me. It hadn't been a dream. That had been the first temptation. If I had gone for that treasure...

"Traxia summoned the kraken to avenge her mother and punish my father for abandoning them. She believed he should have married her mother and made her queen of Llys instead of my Aunt Eira."

"She wanted her parents to have the same arrangement your grandparents had!"

"Exactly," Erik nodded. "Traxia went into hiding after her crime, because she knew our aunt, Queen Eira, would have her executed, too. In the four years after that, she terrorized our shores and any ship that crossed our waters. Queen Eira helped me defeat her. However, she felt death was too kind a punishment for Traxia who had killed her brother, undermined her reign, and trampled our peace treaty. Instead, she imprisoned Traxia in the very psyche her mother had used to torture mine. There, Traxia would linger eternally, unless I showed mercy and set her free."

"That voice... That was your sister?" I asked, already knowing the answer.

"Yes."

"But how? Surely your aunt wouldn't have set you up with such a curse?"

"She didn't. My first wife caused all of this."

My jaw dropped. Of all the answers I could have imagined, this wasn't what I expected.

"Contrary to popular belief, I didn't return cursed from defeating the kraken. I didn't kill it. I only weakened it enough that the Llysians' sea witches could get it back under their control. Everything was fine. As soon as the threat to our seas had passed, our allies pressured me to marry, so I did."

"Yes, I remember the extravagant festivities. Everyone talked about Queen Sacha's beauty and grace," I said pensively.

Erik snorted with a disgusted expression. "That pretty face hid an incredibly spoiled child. Sacha was as nosy as she was greedy. She had convinced herself there were treasures in the room beyond the Sealed Door. Despite my repeated warnings, she snooped until she found the nautilus key and opened the door. Traxia mesmerized her and used her as a vessel to wreak havoc. Once the connection is established, it cannot be undone and only grows in strength. If Sacha had lived, Traxia would have eventually taken over her body and roamed free again."

I pulled my hand from his grasp and stood up swiftly, putting distance between us. He gaped at me, startled by what he likely perceived as a knee-jerk reaction. But panic was swelling within me.

"She made a connection with me earlier," I said, hating the trembling of my voice. "What are you saying? All is lost for me? You're going to have to put me down, too?"

He blinked at me, then shook his head. "No. No, my darling. It's not like that. She didn't make a connection with you. She simply lured you with her siren's song. You never surrendered control to her." He gestured to the couch. "Please sit down. Everything is okay, Astrid. You have nothing to fear."

My eyes searched his, assessing his honesty. When he held

my gaze unwaveringly, some of the tension knotting my back faded. With shaky steps, I returned to the couch and sat back down, still staring at him with concern. He smiled and extended a hand towards me. I looked at it, hesitating before placing mine in his. He gave it a squeeze, his face melting with gratitude.

"My first wife released Traxia. Therefore, only my wife can reseal the door. Until all twelve seals are reactivated, anyone exposed to her whispers long enough can fall under her spell."

Pulling away from him again, I stood by the fireplace, my eyes lost in the flickering flames. I heard him approach me. His spicy scent teased my nose before the warmth of his body pressed against my back. Erik wrapped his arms around me, and I leaned back into him.

"I don't want to lose you, Astrid." Pain filled his voice. "I swore I wouldn't allow myself to care for you, but I do. You have burrowed so deep into my heart, the thought of a future without you is tearing me apart. I have tried to distance myself from you, but you're all I can think about, all I want. When I saw you in front of that door…"

Erik turned me around and cupped my face with both hands. I couldn't believe the words coming out of his mouth. Words I had longed to hear, especially over the past weeks when he had closed himself off from me.

"I love you, Astrid. There cannot be any other. I won't survive losing you. Please, my darling, please be strong. You have come so far… I can't…"

Tears slipped down my cheeks, but I was smiling at hearing the blessed words. "I love you too, Erik. You will not lose me. I didn't know who my enemy was before, but I do now. She will not fool me twice."

"My love," he whispered.

He captured my lips in a passionate kiss, and then carried me to bed.

CHAPTER 9

ERIK

After one long and passionate kiss, I released Astrid with much reluctance. The stares of the servants and the guards weighed heavily on us. I didn't need to look at them to know how stunned they felt about such an open display of affection. While I'd always gone out of my way to be kind to my previous wives, I had zealously shielded my heart from ever falling for any of them. When it came to Astrid, that ship had long sailed.

I gently caressed her cheek, reveling in the love with which she gazed upon me. By the Gods, I couldn't lose this woman.

"I will see you later, my darling," I said in a soft tone.

She nodded with a smile. Unable to resist, I brushed my lips against hers one last time before helping her up onto her mount. Astrid waved me goodbye before riding off to the greenhouse. I remained there, staring at her receding back until she faded from view.

When I turned to face Tormund, who was standing a few steps away from me, I caught the expressions of the guards and servants, staring at me with pity. That infuriated me. I didn't care that history gave them every reason to think Astrid would fail as well.

"Keep your pessimistic thoughts to yourself," I snapped to the help, startling them. "If you cannot control your emotions in the presence of the Queen, then I do not need you here!"

They paled, shame and guilt settling on their features, while Tormund glared at them, both outraged and livid. With a sharp flick of his wrist, he indicated for them to leave at once. They scampered off with their heads bowed.

"Apologies, your Majesty. I will see that they are properly disciplined," Tormund said, looking both embarrassed and dismayed.

I waved a dismissive hand. "Just make sure only positive people are allowed around the Queen. She carries a heavy enough burden without having to deal with this nonsense," I said in a clipped tone.

"I will make sure of it, your Majesty."

"Cancel all my audiences today. I'll be gone for a few hours. Alone..."

He stiffened, his usual curiosity mixed with unease flitting over his features. As much as I trusted Tormund—and I did—some things were better left unsaid. One day, I would confess to him what I was up to when I vanished without guards, and without sharing my destination or purpose.

"Very well, your Majesty. Should we expect your return tonight?" he asked.

"Of course," I replied, my expression making it clear I didn't understand why he would assume otherwise. "I will not leave the Queen alone in the castle at night. I will be back before dinner."

He bowed and left briskly. I headed to my study and pressed on a few inconspicuous stones in a specific sequence to open the door to the secret passage. The wall parted revealing a long corridor, wide enough for four people to walk side by side. Despite the distance, I could already smell the salty scent of the ocean. Magical gems embedded in the stone walls at equal distance from each other bathed the passage in a dreamy light, sparing me the need of a torch or having to light sconces along the way.

After a little less than a ten-minute walk, natural light flooded the end of the tunnel, the sound of the wind and the waves ahead indicating I was nearing my destination. I emerged onto a beach in a secret cove and followed the shore up an incline to the left, towards the rocky formation that enclosed the area. I entered a little cave—if it could even be called that. It opened on two sides. I'd entered through the first one. The second one gave directly onto the ocean with the water a couple of meters below.

I stripped out of my clothes, stacking them neatly on an outcropping of rocks, which formed a natural shelf, then returned to the edge. Without hesitation, I dove into the water. Seconds before I hit the water, my nictitating membranes closed over my eyes to protect them. Despite it still being late summer, the coldness of the water bit my skin. I ignored it, closing my legs tightly together, and stretching my arms before me. A stabbing sensation ran down the length of my inner thighs as they fused together to form my tail, while a pinching one clawed at my neck as my gills opened.

I began undulating under the water as my tail finished forming, propelling me forward. Bracing, I inhaled through my gills, my teeth clenched to silence a painful hiss at the normal searing burn of the first few breaths underwater. As a hybrid—and a second generation one at that—I could only form a superficial layer of scales. It wouldn't do much in terms of protecting me from attacks, injuries, or parasites. However, it helped reduce water resistance when I swam, allowing me to achieve record speeds.

My discomfort waned as my body temperature regulated itself to function in this new environment, as did the impression of suffocating. My lungs always procrastinated at switching to this new method of breathing, mostly because I used it too rarely since the death of my father. As welcoming as the Llysians had always been with me, I always felt a little out of place in their midst.

As with every time I traveled to Llys, my heart constricted over the untimely loss of my sire. I had never been too close to my mother, in large part because the mirror had kept her too enthralled, not to mention the countless miscarriages which had sent her down a spiral of depression. But our secret nature had also brought my father and me closer. While I didn't have as strong an affinity with water as he did, I had loved spending time harpoon fishing underwater with him in the traditional ways of the Llysians or exploring the aquatic realm while honing my unique abilities.

I swam through a massive school of fish. They didn't scatter, some of them even came to swim alongside for a short while. Another pang of sorrow constricted my chest, remembering how my father had taught me to communicate with sea life, especially aquatic mammals, and the games we played with them.

I wished I could share similar moments with Astrid. She would never have gills like a Llysian—or a hybrid like my father and me. However, there were ways to allow a human to breathe underwater. After all, that was what had permitted my grandfather and Queen Alinor to get together. A powerful longing swept through me at the thought of bringing my wife before the Llysian throne, to present our firstborn to his or her other people.

Would our child share my abilities?

I wanted to believe it. But I wouldn't find out until the curse was lifted. No wife of mine—and more broadly, no queen in Rathlin—would ever be able to conceive so long as the psyche's evil magic continued to seep through the door. Only a complete seal would end its vile effects. If we didn't stop Traxia, she would effectively put an end to my bloodline.

The soft, glowing lights of Llys appearing in the distance chased away these somber thoughts. I would never tire of the mesmerizing spectacle of Llysians swimming around in a graceful dance. They always made it look so effortless. But it was also the beautiful colors of their iridescent scales that made it look even more magical. They came in every shade, their hair matching the color of their tail, with their skin being a paler hue of it.

Like them, my tail had the same midnight blue color as my hair. However, my skin didn't have a paler shade of blue. A good thing, too, as it would have made passing myself off as a human completely impossible. I waved at a few familiar faces who either waved back or greeted me with ultrasonic songs.

I had no problems emitting ultrasonic clicks to echolocate a target or assess my environments, but my underwater siren song fell short. While I could entice and control most aquatic mammals using it, I had little effect on Llysians, whether in the water or on solid ground. However, humans I had no problem putting under my compulsion.

I headed straight for the palace, ignoring the beautiful buildings, which deceptively looked like elaborate coral reefs from a distance. Humans would have long drowned before they could have gotten close enough to actually see the complex architecture of the city. The guards nodded at me as I swam up the entrance into the great hall. I emerged from the water, my tail unraveling as I closed the distance with the short flight of stairs to the main floor.

My gills resealed shut, and my first breath through my nose made me dizzy. It always felt like an excessive influx of oxygen after the scarcer one through my gills. My hands resting on top of the first step, my body still in the water, I took a moment to regain my bearings before hoisting myself out. I climbed the handful of steps while squeezing the excess water out of my hair.

Although no one would blink at anyone traipsing around fully nude, Llysians almost always wore some form of clothing, mainly around their genitals, and usually a skirt. Females didn't cover their breasts, which were generally smaller than those of an average woman. Thankfully, a series of shelves at the entrance of the great hall offered skirts in every size and style for anyone to use. I picked one up and wrapped it around my waist as I padded along the pale stone tiles paving the room and into the hallway.

I nodded at the people traipsing around as I made my way towards the throne room. Before I could reach it, an enticing, throaty voice called out my name from the left side of the room.

"Erik. We've been waiting for you," Inga said.

I glanced in her direction and found her standing near the guarded staircase leading to the menagerie. At fifty-nine years old, the Royal Sea Witch barely looked a day older than twenty-eight. She had pale brown skin, with bronze and gold scales, matching her coppery brown hair. Her yellow eyes seemed to glow against her tan skin. Inga was smiling in her usual unreadable way that always gave the impression she knew an incredibly juicy secret.

She signaled for me to come over with a wave of her long and slender fingers. Like most of the other Llysians, she was naked but for an ornate white and gold skirt that fell to the middle of her thighs. Where my scales fully vanished when I unraveled my tail to walk on two legs, pureblood Llysians like her always had theirs.

As was standard with her people, Inga's scales were much thinner over her chest and the dark circles of her nipples before tapering off below her neck. Unlike me, when out of the water, the Llysians' gills on each side of their necks remained fully visible, whereas mine sealed shut into barely noticeable lines. Observed up close, one would easily mistake my closed gills for faded scars.

"Waiting for me, have you?" I asked as I closed the distance with her.

She nodded, her eyes studying my features as if they would

reveal my own secrets. "I could feel your unrest—not to say your distress. Eira is below. Come."

Not waiting for me to respond, Inga immediately started down the stairs. My brow creased, wondering what her magic had gathered, but I complied with her request. While Llysians observed a fairly strict hierarchy, they didn't bother with formalities like humans. They addressed everyone by their first names, even Queen Eira. No one walked around mentioning their titles at every turn.

We descended into the bowels of the castle, the stone walls giving way to reinforced glass walls behind which they held the fearsome kraken. Much farther down the hallway to the side, other battle creatures were held, each in their individual enclosures.

The kraken's enormous eyes—each one bigger than my head —immediately glowed when it saw me. It came closer, its massive tentacles swiping over the reinforced glass. Some of its suction cups pulsated as if it was attempting to smell me through the wall separating us.

"Dear nephew, you've come at last," Queen Eira said.

I forced my gaze away from my nemesis to pay my respects. She was the spitting image of her mother, my grandmother Queen Alinor. From her, we had both inherited the midnight blue hair and silver eyes.

"Hello, Aunt Eira. Why does it sound like you were both expecting me?" I asked before gently kissing her cheek.

"Because we were, of course," she replied before caressing my beard. "Frankly, seeing how agitated the kraken was last night, we were bracing for terrible news."

"And they almost were," I said grimly before relating how Traxia had nearly tricked Astrid.

Inga frowned as she reflected on my words. "Traxia is getting more creative and elaborate in her deceptions. Your wife must be presenting her with some serious resistance."

"Astrid has been handling this so much better than I ever imagined she could," I said, my heart torn between admiration and the fear of losing her. "The first four months, it almost felt like she didn't even feel Traxia's presence."

"Which is truly impressive. It takes a tremendous amount of mental fortitude to resist the siren's call of a sea witch," Inga mused out loud before casting a questioning look at me. "Does she have any magical blood in her ancestry?"

I shook my head. "Not that I know of. Astrid can look demure, almost timid at times. But when you least expect it, she displays great strength and an assertiveness you'd never think she possessed. She exceeded everything I hoped for."

"So I see," Aunt Eira said. "She's lasted nearly five months already. Either you're doing something right, or you're choosing stronger wives."

I grunted and waved a dismissive hand before going to stand before the kraken. It further pressed itself against the glass separating us. As a child, such proximity terrified me. How could mere glass, reinforced though it was, protect us from this almost godly force of nature, with incredible powers over the elements? My father telling me that the sea witches' enchantments prevented the beast from attacking had failed to convince me. How could a witch's magic control such a being?

And yet...

"I'm certainly not doing anything right. Frankly, I'm not doing anything. The past month has grown increasingly difficult for Astrid. All I can do is sit there, and helplessly watch while Traxia is slowly driving her insane."

I turned back to face them, making no effort to hide the despair eating me from within.

"Month after month, year after year, I have accepted that I would be forever trapped in this endless cycle of torment and death," I spit out, anger and anguish simmering inside me. "I made my peace with the fact that I would be the last of my line as no bride could defeat Traxia. But I won't be able to do this anymore."

"Erik! What are you saying?" my aunt asked, the tension in her face reflecting the one in her voice.

"Exactly what I just said; I can't do this anymore. I've tried to be a good husband to each of my former wives and gave them as much happiness as I possibly could in what limited time they had left. In every single one of those balls, I chose the next maiden who would die, performed my duties for however long she lasted, and appropriately mourned her after chopping her head off. But not with Astrid."

"She's not dead yet, son," Eira argued.

"YET!" I shouted. "Not dead *yet*! Neither of you think she will make it. You expect me to just keep going through the motions, behead her when she fails, and then start over with another."

"We all have our duties," Eira said in a stern voice, her face closing off.

"I SPIT ON YOUR DUTIES! I *will not* do this anymore," I hissed.

"Very well," Inga said in that haughty tone I so hated. "Don't do it anymore. Then what? You're going to sail off into the sunset to lick your wounds while the population of Rathlin and of Llys gets decimated by Traxia and the kraken?"

"No," I said in a tired voice, my anger fading as quickly as it had sparked, leaving me cold and empty. "The gods willing, this time, I will die with her."

Both females paled, shock and disbelief etched on their faces.

"You cannot mean this!" Eira whispered.

I didn't respond and merely held her gaze, my eyes giving her the confirmation she sought.

"He does," Inga replied in my stead, understanding dawning on her. "You're in love with your wife."

I closed my eyes and heaved a pained sigh before turning away from them. A thousand burning swords stabbed at my heart at the thought of the fate that awaited Astrid.

"I can't lose her. I won't survive losing her... not her."

Eira's bare feet shuffled lightly on the stone floor before her cool hand gently caressed the back of my shoulder.

"Oh, son, I'm so sorry," my aunt said, her voice filled with compassion.

My anger wanted to surge again. I had no use for her sympathy. We needed solutions, concrete measures we could use to thwart Traxia's relentless assault.

"I cannot begin to imagine how difficult all of this is for you," Eira continued in a soothing voice. "You know I'd do anything to help if I could. Erik, you're my brother's only son, and I love you like you were my own child. But—"

"But nothing," I interrupted, spinning around to face her. "If you love me, help me! Help *us*! With all this magic, surely there is more that you can do to silence Traxia's voice? There must be some talisman or trinket—"

"We *can't* do that, Erik. You know better," my aunt said, interrupting me this time. "*We* cannot interfere. This is *her* challenge to overcome. Any talisman or magic we use will break the covenant, and Traxia will automatically be free. You *know* that. I'd give anything for this nightmare to end. What you may not realize is that I also cannot have an heir either until this curse is lifted. I am a Queen of Rathlin as well."

I recoiled, rendered speechless by this confession. Considering the Llysians' low reproduction rate, I'd always assumed that had been the cause of her lack of offspring, not the curse.

"But... How? The cursed psyche is inside the dungeon," I argued.

"But the kraken is here," Eira replied in a factual tone before casting a brief glance at the creature, still staring intently at me. "So long as his blood bond with Traxia endures, I will remain barren. Do not doubt that I want this over as much as you do. The only thing that can be done is for you to remain steadfast by her side. Lend her your strength when she needs it. Let the love you feel for her be a reminder of what she fights for."

My heart sank a bit more with each of her words. I had known coming here that this would be her answer. Had there been a different solution, she would have shared it with me years ago. Now, knowing how the curse also affected her, and how helpless she, too, remained further crushed me.

"I can't lose her," I repeated in a broken voice.

"Oh son," she whispered again, pulling me into her embrace.

I buried my face in her hair, fighting back the tears that pricked my eyes. My throat painfully constricted, I listened to her humming a sweet melody while caressing my hair, the vibration in her siren voice soothing me at a bone-deep level. For a moment, I almost felt like a little boy again when my mother would console me. Those days of happiness and normalcy had been far too brief before she steadily declined into madness.

"There might be something that you could do," Inga suddenly said in a hesitant voice.

My head jerked up, and I peered at her with an impossible hope blossoming in my heart. My aunt partially released me to stare inquisitively at her sea witch over her shoulder.

"You have true love for her, yes?" Inga asked.

"I do," I replied with conviction. "My heart and soul are hers. There can be no one else."

"Does *she* love *you*?" Inga asked.

I blinked, taken aback by that question. "Yes, I believe she does."

"Has your wife ever said it? Has her behavior displayed it?" she insisted.

I frowned, baffled by this line of questioning. "Yes, she has said it. The way she looks at me, touches me, and interacts with me confirms it. There is no doubt in my mind that Astrid does love me."

"Perfect, then use it to counter Traxia's attacks," Inga replied.

"What does that even mean?" I asked, getting irritated by her vagueness. "How am I supposed to use the feelings my wife and I share against Traxia?"

"By using your compulsion on Astrid whenever Traxia tries to tempt her."

I stiffened. "Are you crazy?"

"Inga! You know perfectly well that he cannot do that! Astrid must resist temptation with her own will. Erik cannot force her to ignore Traxia's siren song, whether physically or otherwise."

"Nor am I asking him to," Inga said calmly. "You cannot use your voice to tell her not to open the Sealed Door, or to tell her to block out Traxia's voice. But you *can* give her a different compulsion to focus on—one she has no reason or desire to fight. Yielding to something you want is easy. Make it something that feeds into happy moments the two of you share, which doesn't have to be sex. When forced to decide between obeying Traxia's command and or spending a pleasant moment with the man she loves, the choice will be easier. And that *choice* will remain entirely hers."

My lips parted, and my eyes widened in understanding. "You're brilliant. Of course, I can do that!" I whispered, my heart soaring.

"But I must warn, Erik, that you cannot abuse this," Inga cautioned. "It will create a mental strain that could break Astrid. Do not come too forcefully at her. Coax her away. Retreat if needed to give her some time to breathe, then gently tug again. You cannot hammer her with your compulsion."

I frowned and nodded slowly. "I understand."

"Only use it when needed. And if at all possible, entice Astrid from the beginning, as soon as Traxia attempts to lure her, while the temptation is still weak," Inga further explained.

"I will keep that in mind. Thank you," I said with sincere gratitude.

"Yes, thank you," Aunt Eira said, looking affectionately at her sea witch.

"This is only an extra tool," Inga once more cautioned. "Your real power is the love you share. Just be there for her and support her in all the ways you can."

"I will. Thanks again," I replied.

The kraken waving his tentacles over the glass wall reclaimed my attention. His eyes glowed in an accrued intensity as it stared at me.

"You want to kill me, don't you?" I asked in a teasing tone.

"No, he doesn't," Aunt Eira replied in his stead, sounding amused. "His crippled bond with Traxia is making him distressed. Normally, he just sulks around. But your presence triggers him. Not because Traxia deems you her enemy, but because you share the same blood, *and* you defeated him."

"What?" I asked, stunned.

"Traxia and you have the same father. Your blood is similar enough that he wants to bond with you instead," Eira explained. "You also bested him, which makes him your servant."

"Then why is he a threat to the realm and cursing you?" I challenged.

"Because Traxia still holds power over him. Defeat her, and you will truly be the Sea King of Rathlin Islands, with the kraken at your command."

CHAPTER 10
ASTRID

The weeks that followed seriously tested me. After that fateful night, Traxia's voice became a loud and obnoxious constant companion. Despite my determination not to fall prey to her compulsion, the lure of her siren's call was nearly impossible to resist. It was only a matter of time before I surrendered to its summoning. Thankfully, I was never alone anymore, day or night. While the servants still kept their distance, Tormund ensured someone always had me in their line of sight when within the castle walls. This couldn't work in the long term. With six more months to go, I had to find another way.

During the day, Traxia used to be reasonably quiet, focusing her attacks at night when sleep made me more vulnerable. But she's been gradually escalating her assaults to the point of becoming relentless. Having Erik near me always made things easier, especially when he spoke to me with that altered pitch in his voice. It drowned out everything else. I believed he had some kind of siren voice, too.

But as always, he was meeting with nobles—local and foreign—and holding court. I hated that I couldn't be by his side. It always made me feel like a shameful secret. But people became distracted by my presence. And frankly, I hated the constant looks of pity and the morbid curiosity with which people stared at me.

However, if Traxia didn't shut up, I would go insane. I hated the sound of her voice in my head, constantly whispering my name, or humming nursery rhymes in a tauntingly creepy fashion. She wasn't even trying to lure me to the Sealed Door. She was merely trying to drive me crazy, to break my will so that she could then do with me as she pleased.

With an aggravated grunt, I tossed my embroidery on the couch and jumped to my feet before storming out of my boudoir. The servant that had conveniently been lurking outside the room immediately stiffened, worry etched on her face upon noticing my demeanor. Although I paid her little attention, I didn't miss her relief when I headed towards the exit of the castle rather than towards the dungeon.

The guards pushed open the massive doors of the castle as soon as they saw me approach. After only a few steps outside, the vise-like pressure that had been crushing my mind suddenly loosened its grip by at least half. I could have wept with relief. Wanting more—needing more—I half ran a few meters away from the building, each step providing me with a bit more relief.

And then it struck me.

A million thoughts flooded my mind as the solution to my woes finally came to me. I'd been wondering why the first four months had been so easy and why the last couple had grown increasingly difficult. Of all Erik's previous wives, Ariana had lasted significantly longer than the others. I couldn't figure out what she and I might have had in common to explain our performance. The answer was so obvious, I now felt like a complete idiot for not having seen it sooner.

Like me, Ariana also loved the outdoors. She had been an artist and spent most of her days painting in the garden or in one of the courtyards. She would often walk in the woodlands on the castle grounds, looking for birds and other small wild creatures to sketch. While the colder season had driven her back indoors, my greenhouse needing much less maintenance with most of my plants slowly maturing, I'd had little reason to leave the castle as often.

Within a fortnight of staying more frequently inside, Ariana had fallen. No wonder the servants didn't sleep within the castle. They, too, would fall victim to constant exposure.

My mind racing, I glanced around the domain. I couldn't spend all of my days sitting inside the greenhouse, staring at the plants growing. Anyway, fall was already around the corner. Soon, it would be too cold for me to seek refuge there. I couldn't stay away from the castle for extended periods, so I needed a warm and comfortable place outside the building but within its grounds where I could spend my days.

Unfortunately, unlike some other foreign castles, Rathlin didn't have a queen's pavilion. I couldn't go sit in the stables, and even less in the carriage hangar. What else was there?

The hunters' pavilion!

My eyes widened in shock as my heart soared. Unwilling to get back inside just yet and be subjected to more of Traxia's abuse, I asked a guard to go fetch Tormund. By the swiftness with which the majordomo appeared, I realized he'd been lurking nearby. The servant had undoubtedly warned him of my hasty escape from my boudoir. It both warmed my heart to have so many people watching over me, but also made me feel trapped. For someone who enjoyed her privacy, being constantly spied on felt suffocating. And yet, in this instance, if it could help me make it through this horrible year, I welcomed it.

"Your Highness?" Tormund asked as soon as he reached me.

Despite his efforts at hiding his emotions, I didn't miss his underlying air of concern. Like the servants, the older man was doing his best not to allow a friendship to blossom between us. After twenty-seven queens, he had every reason to shelter himself from growing attached to Erik's latest wife. And yet, in his role, more than any other, he had no choice but to frequently interact with me. Despite his politely distant behavior, I'd grown fond of him. And I could tell he was losing his battle at remaining indifferent to me. At first, I thought it was merely out of concern for his king. But I genuinely believed Tormund was also starting to care about me.

"Do I correctly understand that the hunters' pavilion is currently unused?" I asked.

Tormund blinked, clearly taken aback by the unexpected question. "Yes, your Majesty. The king hasn't held any hunts in quite a few years."

He didn't have to specify that they ended when the curse began.

"Excellent. Would it be possible to have it refreshed and ready for use as soon as possible?" I asked in a nonchalant tone. "I could use a change of scenery, and with the fall quickly approaching, the greenhouse will get too cool to spend time there."

Tormund's eyes widened with sudden understanding. He cast an almost stunned look at the castle, as if wondering why he hadn't thought of it himself, before returning his attention to me.

"It will be done at once, your Majesty," Tormund replied with an uncharacteristic eagerness for someone usually very stoic. "If there's anything specific you would like moved there or that you would like us to acquire on your behalf, I'll make sure it is brought there for you."

"Thank you, Tormund," I said warmly.

"No, your Majesty. Thank *you*."

My throat tightened at the way he spoke those words. For the first time, he had dropped his cool and professional mask. Although it was brief, the almost paternal look he gave me touched me beyond words. I terribly missed my father. While I understood his reasons to keep his distance, they didn't hurt any less. As much as I respected his need to protect himself and my sister by mourning me in advance, I also resented that lack of support. How could he not comprehend that I had a greater chance of succeeding with my loved ones by my side, reminding me of everything I needed to continue fighting for?

Efficient as ever, Tormund had an army of servants and groundskeepers working on the hunters' pavilion within the hour. Located at the edge of the woodlands, it was far enough from the castle to give me a pleasant reprieve, but close enough not to trigger the distance offensive mechanism like if I would spend too much time in town.

Within two days, they had thoroughly cleaned, repainted, and refurnished. I'd even decorated it with fresh flowers picked from the greenhouse. The peace it offered was beyond wonderful, with Traxia's voice nothing more than a dull echo in the back of my mind, if I heard her at all.

Vast and luxurious, it rivaled the cottages of many nobles in town. The large arched windows all around the octagonal sitting room let the sunlight flood inside the room. I'd elected to settle here and have my desk set up near the large fireplace that would keep the room warm once the season changed. A decent sized kitchen and larder provided for my needs should I go hungry.

Always thinking of everything, Tormund had turned the armory into a music room and brought in a second harp as he knew my passion for that instrument. But the most thoughtful gesture had been to turn one of the other rooms into a bedroom so that I could rest if needed. With Traxia making my life impossible at night, I'd taken to napping during the day to catch up on the sleep she kept depriving me of.

When I had requested to reopen the hunting pavilion, I had not expected anyone to go out of their way to make it this welcoming. I had just wanted it cleaned and comfortable—a quiet and warm place where I could kill time away from my tormentor.

For all his stoicism and reserved behavior, Tormund had a heart of gold. Granted, he was first and foremost devoted to his king and wanted to see Erik freed of this curse. But it went beyond that.

Settling behind the ornate wooden desk, I picked up a piece of parchment to write a letter to my sister. Those exchanges with her made me feel less isolated. Not wanting to worry her more than necessary, I'd been reluctant to confess how taxing my challenge had become over the past few weeks. I'd just begun telling her of the blissful peace the pavilion provided when my husband paid me an unexpected visit.

"Erik!" I exclaimed, jumping from my seat. "I thought you would be in meetings for many more hours."

My pulse always fluttered whenever I saw him. Although he still kept some secrets, he no longer kept his heart from me. Since that dreadful night when Traxia almost tricked me into opening the door, Erik stopped fighting his growing feelings for me. And that, more than anything else, gave me the strength to see this mess through. I wanted to be his perfect queen, to stand by his side rather than remain in the shadows. I wanted to travel with him, to plan a future together, and have many children with his stunning silver eyes.

He smiled and shook his head as he closed the distance between us. "I was supposed to, but I got rid of them. They were boring me with their constant demands and complaints. Plus, I missed my wife, and I wanted to see your new lair."

I melted when he drew me into his embrace, his lips settling on mine with a possessive tenderness that had my blood instantly heating. The kiss deepened, his hands caressing a path up my back before settling on my nape. A sliver of disappointment coursed through me when Erik broke the kiss rather than unleash his usual passion on me.

"How are you feeling," he asked, his gentle voice laced with a bit of concern.

A radiant smile stretched my lips. "I feel absolutely wonderful. It's been a few weeks since I've felt this good."

A powerful emotion that crossed his features. My throat tightened at the sight of this vulnerable expression on such a strong man.

"I've failed you in so many ways," he said in a pained voice. "I should have thought of it first. Instead, I let you suffer—"

I pressed two fingers to his lips and gave him a stern look. "You didn't fail me, Erik. The only thing that has made this whole thing bearable is you. The way you looked at me when you walked in, the way you hold me and kiss me, your kindness and generosity... Nobody has ever made me feel as precious as you do. My own father has turned his back on me and is keeping Kara away. You have been my one steadfast support, the pillar that has kept me standing strong through this ordeal. Don't you dare berate yourself. If not for you, I'd be dead by now."

"But—"

"But nothing," I interrupted him again. "We are a team in this. I don't expect you to have all the answers. If you did, this curse would have been lifted years ago. All that matters is that we're past the six-month mark and well on our way to the seventh. I'm still here, and now I have a new reprieve during the day. And I have you at night to keep me safe. We're going to do this together."

"Together," he repeated before reclaiming my mouth.

Dear Gods, I was truly falling in love with that man. After a few more kisses and caresses, Erik released me, and I gave him a tour of my new refuge.

"As you can see, Tormund and the servants have outdone themselves," I said as we finished touring the music room.

When we entered the bedroom, I studied Erik's features, trying to assess the thoughts crossing his mind as he surveyed the space.

Licking my lips nervously, I squared my shoulders before

sharing the idea I'd been toying with since requesting they reopened this place.

"Although this room is quite humble compared to our bedchamber at the castle, it's quite cozy and comfortable," I said carefully. "Considering how peaceful it is here, would it be acceptable for me to sleep here?"

My heart sank when Erik immediately shook his head. "No, that's not an option."

"Why not?" I asked pleadingly. "I'm still on the castle's grounds, yet far enough that Traxia's lure barely reaches me. Nights are a nightmare at the castle. The temptation is so much more potent, and with the dungeon so close, the risks of her getting me to do her bidding before you or anyone else can intervene is greater. But from here, even if she managed to lure me, the long walk back to the castle would give me a chance to wake up or for you to do so."

Instead of swaying him, each of my words only appeared to make Erik further close himself off.

"In theory, your arguments are valid, but you must return to the castle every night," he said in a firm tone. "The medallion will punish you if you don't."

An icy shiver ran down my spine, and I cast a worried glance at the nautilus-shaped pendant. "Hurt me how? And why? I thought I just needed to be on the castle's grounds."

Erik shook his head again. "There is a link between the door and this medallion. The door feeds energy to the medallion. Distance creates a strain on that bond. The greater the distance, and the faster it dwindles. Since you are not too far from the castle, its energy drains slower, but it still does. Once the link becomes too weak, the medallion will start taking its energy from you."

I felt blood drain from my face, and I swallowed hard. My hand closed around the medallion while my mind raced. Erik had no reason to lie to me about this. But the prospect of returning to the castle gutted me. I didn't want to lose the peace I'd been enjoying over the past few hours.

"Have you tried it with one of the others before?" I asked, clinging to one last hope. I couldn't bring myself to refer to my predecessors as his wives.

"No," Erik reluctantly conceded.

"Then we should at least try," I quickly said when he opened his mouth to state the reasons he felt it wouldn't work. "We're close to the castle. If I'm wrong, we can return in no time. It's not like when I was in the city. But what if I'm right? Five and a half months is still a long time. If there's the slightest chance, we must try it. Please!"

Erik clenched his teeth and shook his head, the movement barely perceptible, and more aimed at himself for even considering it. Everything in his demeanor screamed how strongly he opposed this idea. Closing the short distance between us, I placed my palms on his chest and gave him a pleading look.

"Please, Erik. At least, we'll know," I begged.

He closed his eyes, the tension in his square jaw tightening as he battled with himself. With a frustrated grunt, Erik slowly opened his eyelids, his silver eyes boring into mine.

"Against my better judgement, I will grant you this request only because it is *you* who endures all this pain," he said, sounding almost angry. "But I *know* it won't go well. At the first sign of any discomfort, and if the hue of the lights on your medallion shifts even in the slightest, we will race back to the castle. This also means you will sleep fully dressed."

"Yes, Erik. Thank you!" I said in a breathy voice, before burying my face in his chest and holding him tightly.

Although he returned my embrace, his spine remained stiff. A sense of unease settled in the pit of my stomach at his palpable reluctance. As much as I trusted Erik, I didn't believe my request to be unreasonable.

"Don't thank me. I fear my weakness will only cause you more unnecessary pain," he said grimly.

I lifted my head to look at him. "You're not weak. You're merely helping me explore possible ways of beating this thing. We're in this together. I couldn't do this without you," I said softly.

Erik grunted in a non-committal fashion. I didn't press the matter further for fear he would change his mind, as he clearly wanted to do.

"Can I play some harp for you?" I offered, wanting to move the discussion away from us spending the night here. "I haven't tried the music room yet. It would be more fun with an audience."

Although still troubled by the situation, Erik smiled at me, his face softening in that way I loved. He nodded and let me take his hand to lead him into the room. He sat in a plush chair across from me as I settled on the bench in front of the massive harp. As soon as my fingers began plucking at the cords, the tension between us faded. I loved playing music, and Erik loved listening to me perform. The acoustics of the armory turned into a music room obviously didn't rival those of the castle, but I didn't care. I was alone with my husband, with delightful melodies filling my ears instead of the wretched voice of a bitter sea witch.

An hour before the sun would set, a servant came inquiring if we needed anything. I suspected it was more a matter of Tormund making sure Erik or someone else was keeping an eye on me.

"We will likely spend the night here," Erik replied. "Please have our evening meal brought here."

My stomach knotted when the servant miserably failed to hide her shock, disbelief, and worry at my husband's statement. However, she didn't argue, merely bowed her head, and promptly left. With that, Erik's unease returned.

"So what were the nobles pestering you about earlier?" I asked, wanting to distract him from his somber thoughts.

Not fooled in the least, he gave me a sad smile but played along. Erik extended a hand to me. I gladly took it and let him lead me to the ornate, dark wood couch across from the fireplace, with deep red, plush cushions embroidered with gold threads.

He sat down before pulling me onto his lap. I couldn't get enough of snuggling with him. As much as I hated Traxia's obsessive cruelty, I owed her terrible attack for getting Erik to finally stop closing himself off to me. Granted, he'd always been kind and tender, but having him openly affectionate, seeing his silver eyes spark with love, made me feel cherished and gave me hope for a brighter future. I only had to hang on a little while longer.

"Their usual greedy grievances," Erik replied with a shrug. "They've encountered some competition alongside their favorite trade routes. They want me to forbid access to our waters to any rival, so that they can continue to charge outrageous prices for their goods. Lord Sten even went so far as to ask I release the kraken on any trespassers."

"What?!" I exclaimed, mouth gaping. "That sounds a little excessive."

"More like beyond excessive," Erik said with disgust. "The kraken should only ever be summoned in extreme cases, and even then. It is not easily controlled—least of all this one— unless you have an extremely powerful sea witch who has bonded with it."

I frowned at those words. "Why 'least of all this one'?" I asked.

Erik suddenly looked uncomfortable, which had every one of my senses on high alert. "Traxia's mother raised this kraken. And Traxia also has a blood bond with it," he reluctantly confessed.

My jaw dropped, and I pressed a hand to my chest as a sense of dread washed over me.

"Do not worry, my love. While their bond makes it harder to control the kraken, it doesn't make it impossible. So long as Traxia remains trapped behind the Sealed Door, she cannot summon it to her or make it do her bidding."

It didn't reassure me half as much as I wished it did. To the contrary, it further emphasized just how badly I needed to succeed. The trickle-down effect of my failure went beyond my personal death. It meant another nightmarish round of this endless hell for Erik. Another young maiden subjected to this torture, and the risk of massive bloodshed should Traxia ever go free. With the kraken at her beck and call, she would unleash her wrath on both the people of Rathlin and the merfolk who had cast her out.

A cold shiver ran down my spine at that prospect.

"Then we have to make sure she remains there," I said, trying to sound confident.

"We certainly will," Erik replied, although not fooled in the least. "You've outlasted everyone. And I refuse to lose you. We *will* beat this."

I smiled and lifted my face towards his when he leaned forward. My lips parted as he deepened the kiss, my stomach fluttering with the familiar desire he always awakened in me. My skin heated as his hands immediately began to caress me in a bold fashion. Erik wasn't jesting when he warned me of his healthy sexual appetite. Thankfully, I fully approved of it.

Well, except this time.

My blood heated, and my skin tingled. But as much as I wanted my husband to carry me into the bedroom, we wouldn't be done quickly. With Erik's impressive stamina, he could go for multiple rounds back-to-back. As the servants would be returning soon with our evening meal, we had to delay giving in to our naughty urges to avoid giving them a rather questionable spectacle.

Another shiver coursed through me, and the tingling intensified. Slipping a hand beneath my skirt, Erik caressed a path up my leg and between my thighs to settle on my sex. My breath hitched, and he broke the kiss to stare me in the eyes with a provocative smile.

"We don't have time," I whispered, my lips almost brushing against his.

His smile broadened, a glimmer of defiance shining in his silver eyes. "There's always enough time to pleasure my wife. I want to hear you shout my name."

Before I could respond, he reclaimed my lips, his fingers sneaking into my undergarment, and going straight for my core. I whimpered, as the blood in my veins heated some more, my pelvis lifting to meet his hand as his thumb massaged my little nub while two of his fingers slipped inside me.

Erik knew exactly how to touch me to make me fall apart. I ground on his hand, chasing after the bliss he always gave me. However, even as he expertly rubbed me, I struggled to abandon myself to pleasure. The fire in my veins was growing too hot. The tingling in my skin was starting to feel more like a thousand needles prickling at me. And my shortened breath from excitement had me on the verge of suffocating.

Placing my palms on Erik's shoulders, I pushed him back while turning my head to break the kiss. Not realizing something was off, he grabbed my nape and tried to draw my face back to his. This time, I pushed back more forcefully, while my stomach roiled.

"No! Something's wrong," I said in a strained voice.

Erik's confused expression gave way to horror as he visibly blanched. He wasn't looking at me, but at my chest. Only then did I notice the pink glow between my breasts, mostly hidden by my bodice.

My husband yanked his hand away, picking me up in his arms. The room spun around me as he shot to his feet and dashed for the exit. The reddish hue of the falling night sky no longer looked enchanting and romantic, seeming ominous instead. I felt feverish and as if the heavy weight was pressing increasingly hard, making it a struggle to fill my lungs with enough air. When Erik hoisted me onto his horse, I nearly fell off as spasms coursed through my muscles. He deftly caught me even as he hopped behind me.

Holding me tightly, my back to his chest, Erik set his horse galloping towards the castle at a punishing pace. Tears pricked my eyes, and I swallowed a whimper from the needles stabbing at my flesh. My nerve endings had become so overly sensitive that the soft fabric of my dress felt like glass shards scraping me raw.

"Hang on, my love. We'll be there soon. Hang on," Erik said.

I tried to focus on his voice, but I was drowning in an ocean of agony. For a moment, I nearly screamed for Erik to turn back. Our racing towards the castle didn't seem to dampen the pain as each excruciating symptom kept growing in intensity the more the daylight faded. The pulsating glow from the medallion going from the light pink to an angry red.

And then just like that, it stopped.

The weight on my chest lifted so abruptly, I feared my chest would explode from my lungs so suddenly filling with air. Simultaneously, the searing heat burning me from the inside out vanished in a blink, leaving me almost chilled as goosebumps erupted all over my skin. The stabbing needles also relented, although my skin still felt tenderized. No visible line or landmark revealed the reason for this change. I could only presume we'd crossed a proximity threshold, which disabled the medallion's attack mechanism.

"It stopped," I whispered. "The pain is gone."

Erik stretched his neck to look at my medallion. Despite the lingering haze from the harsh punishment my stubborn defiance had wrought, I didn't miss the relief on his face. My husband's arm tightened around my waist while guilt gnawed at me. He had warned me. I had no one but myself to blame for the pain I'd just endured, but it was the distress my insistence had caused him that shamed me the most.

He only started slowing down once we approached the castle. I adjusted my clothes and, like him, I schooled my features to hide from the guards and the staff what had prompted this mad dash back home. Worrying them more than they already were would serve no purpose. Then again, with my horse still back at the hunting pavilion, and Erik having left the door wide open, the servants wouldn't need a lot of imagination to figure out what might have transpired.

No doubt alerted by the guards, Tormund rushed out of the castle to greet us even as our horse was trotting up to the entrance. Professional as ever, he kept a neutral expression. However, I knew him well enough now to see the sliver of worry in his eyes.

"Your Majesties, you've returned," Tormund said matter-of-factly as Erik stopped the horse a couple of meters in front of him.

He gracefully hopped down from our mount before helping me down. By the way he looked at me, I guessed his silent question. Although I still felt a little wobbly on my legs, I gave him a reassuring smile. Erik smiled back and wrapped his arm around my waist for additional support. Him carrying me inside would have had the tongues wagging even more.

He cast a calm glance at Tormund. "Yes, we have decided to come home for the night. Please have someone retrieve the Queen's horse from the pavilion. We will also have dinner in our room."

"Very well, my king," Tormund said with a slight bow of the head as Erik started leading me inside.

As soon as our bedchamber's door closed behind us, Erik dropped his mask of stoicism to look at me with a devastated expression.

"I'm so very sorry, Astrid, for putting you through this. I knew better than to let you stay away from the castle. If only I'd insisted…"

"No, Erik! No. This is *not* your fault. Do *not* berate yourself over my own stubbornness," I said forcefully. I closed the distance between us and placed my palms on his chest, my gaze boring into his. "You warned me. I made a conscious choice. While I definitely *never* want to go through this again, I'm not sorry we tested it. Now we know. I'm just sorry for putting *you* through this, although I couldn't have done it without you."

"It is my duty to protect you from the things I can, Astrid," Erik argued. "What *I* endure is nothing compared to the trial that monster is putting you through."

I cupped his cheeks and looked at him with affection. "It's only been six months for me, but years for you. Do not dismiss the depth of your pain. It is as much my duty to protect you as it is yours to protect me. Now we know for sure."

"I can't lose you, Astrid," Erik said in a tortured voice.

"You won't. I told you that there would never be another portrait after mine on that wall. I meant it. It will be you and me, until the end," I said with fervor.

"You and me, always."

CHAPTER 11
ERIK

Despite Astrid's arguments, I continued to internally berate myself for allowing her to risk her life like this. Granted, it served us well now knowing beyond any doubt the limits she needed to abide by in terms of being at the castle by nightfall. But I should have listened to my instincts. The speed at which she had deteriorated had terrified me. Had we been alone one kilometer farther away, the Gods only knew if we would have returned in time.

I didn't want to smother Astrid or make her feel controlled or even more imprisoned than was already the case. And yet, I would carry my wife's resentment if needed to keep her safe.

At least, the hunters' pavilion had been a blessing. Two weeks ago, we'd said farewell to October and to Astrid's time in the greenhouse. With the first snowflakes making an appearance —most of them melting the same day—the cold would have forced her to remain in the castle. Instead, the pavilion was truly providing her with wonderful relief during the day.

Nights had become the real challenge. Whatever mischief we denied Traxia during the day, she more than made up for at night. Inga's suggestion that I use my compulsion on Astrid had also been a blessing. I strived to catch Traxia's siren song early, so that I could distract my mate right away. And it worked perfectly. But that also meant me opening myself to my sister's compulsion.

As a Llysian hybrid, I mostly could block or dampen the impact of their siren's song on me if I so chose. That explained why I could remain in the castle without succumbing to her lure, unlike the rest of the servants. But in order to support my wife, I had to let my guard down and open myself up. It had taken Traxia a while to realize that I no longer blocked her. Although she had always been able to telepathically communicate with me, she hadn't been able to mess with my head.

Now, she started doing it.

My sister didn't understand that I welcomed it. While she was busy with me, it granted Astrid a reprieve. The problem was that the more she used her compulsion and illusions on me, the harder it became to differentiate them from reality. At first, they'd had a dreamy glow about them that made it obvious I was seeing things. But lately, I had to briefly block her in order to see the world through my own eyes and make certain what was true and what wasn't.

However, even that she took away from me.

I woke up with a start. Confused, it took me a moment to regain my bearings and realize that Astrid was no longer in our bed. The door stood wide open, the flames from the fireplace casting ominous dancing shadows through the doorway. I carefully glided a hand over where Astrid should be lying. My stomach painfully knotted at finding her spot indeed empty. I couldn't tell for sure if I had stretched my hand in the real world or only in an illusion Traxia might currently have me trapped in.

A muffled scream in the distance startled me—Astrid's scream. I jumped out of bed and grabbed my sleeping tunic from the chair by the door as I ran out of the room. I slipped it on then cast a quick glance at my ring. Thankfully, its gem continued to glow white. That didn't stop my heart from wanting to pound its way out of my chest.

I raced down the stairs just as another scream resonated in the otherwise empty castle. Relief washed over me when the sound emanated from a room far away from the dungeon.

"ASTRID!" I shouted, hoping she would hear me.

Nothing.

I rushed to her boudoir, to my study, and then to the chapel. When I failed to find her in any of those places, I hesitated as to where to look next. The dining room seemed too far from whence the shouts had emanated. But where else...?

"Leave me alone!" Astrid shouted, her muffled voice sounding terrified.

A sense of dread washed over me once I realized it came from the gallery. I should have locked the door. There was no reason for Astrid to be confronted with the faces of my horrible past, and the terrible fate we were desperately fighting to spare her from.

I ran to the gallery and nearly broke the door in my haste to open it. Horror swept over me at the spectacle that awaited me inside. Thunderous clouds rolled overhead where the ceiling should have been. The portraits of my twenty-seven dead wives had come to life, each of them spewing venom at Astrid. Standing in the center of the room in her white nightgown, Astrid was pressing her palms to her ears to block out their voices. Eyes closed, her face drenched in tears, she was vainly trying to free her legs from the corals that had grown out of the hardwood floor, shackling her in place.

"He doesn't love you, foolish girl," Ariana said in a voice full of vitriol. "You may have slightly outlasted me and retained his attention a little longer by a few weeks, but he's tired of you now. Why do you think the first few months were so easy? Erik was protecting you because he enjoyed bedding you. Now, he's ready for you to die so that he can pick a newer, fresher wife."

Blind fury surged through me. Astrid had proven too strong. Despite her multiple efforts or how creative she became with her temptations, Traxia never got Astrid to turn the key clockwise. Every time, that request shattered the illusion. Therefore, my sister's only hope was to destroy Astrid mentally. Once broken and distressed enough, my wife would be easier to manipulate. Undermining our relationship, making her doubt my love and devotion, had been Traxia's main focus since I started using my voice to break her enchantment.

"Astrid! I'm here," I exclaimed, running to her.

She pressed her hands even more tightly against her ears. Eyes closed, she shook her head as if to say she didn't want to be fooled again. I caught her wrists and pulled her hands away from her face. She yelped and jerked her head up to cast a terrified look at me.

"E-Erik?" she asked fearfully.

"Yes, my love. It's me. I'm going to get you out of here."

"No. You're not real. None of this is real," she argued, hope of fear battling within her.

"You're right, my darling. None of this is real, except me. I am real. Let's get out of here," I said gently.

"I can't. My legs," she said in a teary voice, while casting a glance at the corals that kept her rooted in place.

For a second, I considered telling her to will them out of existence. They weren't real. She only had to acknowledge and believe that they weren't there for them to vanish. But seeing how distressed she was, adding that extra strain could cast her down a deadly spiral of madness.

"I will break you free," I pledged.

Cupping her face with both hands, I wiped the tears from her cheeks with my thumbs then gave her a desperate kiss.

I hated how she trembled, but even more how she continued to struggle with believing I wasn't yet another figment of her imagination—or rather of Traxia's illusion.

Releasing her with much reluctance, I ran to one of the decorative armors lining the wall and retrieved its sword.

"You stupid, stupid girl. There is no curse," hissed Sacha, my first wife, as I returned to Astrid. "I didn't set free any sea witch. Erik is using you like he used us. The necklace is sucking out your life force to keep his sister trapped. Without her, he can't control the kraken or the elements."

Another wave of fury surged through me upon hearing those words. I swallowed back the harsh words burning my tongue and focused on my wife. There was no point arguing with an illusion, and least of all with the puppet master pulling the strings behind the curtains.

"Look at me, Astrid," I ordered, altering the pitch of my voice and letting its vibrations initiate the compulsion. "Look at how safely and effectively I am freeing you."

She blinked, seeming slightly confused as she gazed at the coral wrapped around her calves. I raised the sword and started hacking away at her shackles. Fear gave way to hope, as the coral started falling off in large chunks.

"Do not let him make you his next victim," Sacha continued. "You are growing too weak to be of any further use to him. He will sacrifice you to the kraken once you've activated the next seal. Run while you can. Tell the others what is really happening here. This necklace is a trap. Remove it and flee the castle. It will no longer have any hold over you."

I felt my blood drain from my face when Astrid pulled her gaze away from me to stare at the portraits—more specifically at Sacha. Her hand closed around the necklace, and a sliver of doubt flitted over her features. The way she glanced back at me, I realized I was losing her.

"Astrid, come with me, my love. None of this is true," I said pleadingly. "I've freed you. Come with me. Let's get out of this nightmare."

"Remove the necklace and flee," Sacha insisted. "He's trying to trap you. He's using his compulsion on you to keep you from hearing the truth. It is too late for all of us. But it's not too late for you or for his future victims."

Astrid's eyes flicked between mine, searching. Traxia had effectively screwed me over. If I used my voice once more to entice Astrid out of here, it would confirm her accusations.

"I have been by your side for the past eight months, laid my heart bare to you, and showed you in all the ways that I can just how much I love you," I said in my normal voice. "Who does your heart believe?" I waved at the paintings. "This illusion or your husband?"

She wavered, my words appearing to break through without quite convincing her.

"I am not the one who trapped you here to be badgered by ghosts. I'm the one who freed you, who loves you, and who has done everything to protect you," I said in a soothing voice, before resuming my compulsion. "Come to me, my love. It's your choice. It is always *your* choice."

Astrid blinked then stared at the hand I was extending her. For a moment, time stood still, the walls themselves appearing to hold their breaths while waiting for her decision. It took every ounce of my willpower not to shout in victory and relief when she suddenly took on a resolved expression and placed her hand in my hand.

"My love," I whispered with gratitude.

I tossed the sword onto the floor and pulled Astrid after me under the angry voices of the portraits cursing me while telling her what a terrible mistake she was making.

As soon as we exited the room, I slammed the door shut to silence them. But irreversible damage had been done. This seed they had planted would bury deeper, its roots spreading until it choked any trust and love Astrid ever felt for me. We still had a little less than four months remaining. That was a long time to go on facing these escalating attacks. Would she give in to temptation, throw away the necklace, and flee?

I didn't even want to imagine what disaster would follow.

Forcing an enthusiastic expression on my face, I smiled at my wife. "I have a surprise for you. I was saving it for your birthday, but after this ordeal, you could use a bit of cheering up."

"A surprise?" she asked, curiosity replacing some of her distress.

Astrid had never shown herself materialistic or greedy, which made giving her presents all the more agreeable. The way her eyes lit up upon receiving thoughtful presents always moved me. Jewelry or pretty trinkets didn't appeal to her. She accepted them but didn't covet them.

"Yes, it's two parts. I only have the first one here, but it hints at what you will get on your official birthday," I said with a tender smile.

"Very well. You have me intrigued," she said with a timid smile. "Thank you."

However, I didn't miss the glimmer of gratitude in her amber eyes or the way her hand tightened around mine. Astrid wasn't thanking me for the surprise, but for getting her out of that room. We no longer dwelled on these incidents when they occurred, preferring to cast them out as fast as possible not to give them additional power over us.

I squeezed her hand back and let the depth of my feelings for her shine through. "Any time, my darling. I love you, Astrid, with everything that I am."

She smiled, her eyes slightly misting. "I love you, too, Erik."

Astrid's brows shot up when she realized I was taking her to the music room.

"Well, I have a confession to make," I said while opening the door for her. "I didn't have this thick curtain installed on the wall to cover some damage that couldn't be repaired until spring." I waved at the large section of wall between two windows on the left side of the music room.

My wife slightly recoiled, a frown marring her forehead as her gaze flicked between the curtain and me.

"Why would you lie about that?" she asked with a hint of suspicion.

"Actually, I didn't lie. I merely worded things in a way that would make you think I meant repairs. If I recall properly, I said that I was getting some work done there," I amended, kicking myself for raising a topic that would imply—not to say confirm—I'd been deceiving her, as my fake ex-wives claimed.

"Right, I believe those were indeed your words," Astrid replied cautiously, her wariness lingering.

"I didn't want you to look there in order to keep the surprise. As I trusted you not to be nosy, I knew this would be enough," I said. "There is no damage to the wall. The work I was getting done was a long-term project as a surprise for you, to show you how much I love you and how you are all that I see."

Astrid's lips parted, this time, her concern giving way to genuine curiosity and an emotion I couldn't define—but which I loved seeing on her face.

"Wait right here," I said with a smile.

Walking over to the curtain, I pulled it open to reveal the life-size portrait of her, which I had ordered Ogden to paint. However, my heart lurched, and horror descended over me when I didn't find the beautiful image of my smiling wife playing her mother's harp. Instead, I was staring at a painting of the open Sealed Door with me standing inside the room, covered in blood, a sword in my right hand and Astrid's severed head in my left.

"By the Gods," I whispered, swiftly taking a few steps away from the nightmarish vision.

A slow, malevolent laugh rose behind me. I spun around to look at Astrid, grinning maliciously at me.

"A painting of my death at your hands? Really, Erik? That's

the present you have in store for me on the day of my birthday?" she asked, her voice dripping with hatred and contempt.

I froze, robbed of words, my mind refusing to function and failing to make sense of what was happening. And then Astrid started running her fingers through her golden mane, down the luscious curves of her body, before her palms settled on her breasts, fondling them.

"Traxia," I whispered, my stomach roiling with horror as understanding dawned on me.

"I can see why you enjoyed fucking her," she replied, still bearing Astrid's appearance, but now using her own voice. That made me feel even more nauseous. "She's more luscious and curvier than those useless other waifs you handfasted with. I will enjoy using your Astrid's vessel to ride the cock of every male in this realm who I decide to spare. You'll even get to watch, little brother—assuming you don't take your own life first."

"I WILL KILL YOU!" I shouted, taking two menacing steps towards her.

I wanted to bash her head in and tear her limb from limb, but not while she wore Astrid's face. Anyway, this was just an illusion.

"No brother," Traxia said smugly. "I'm not the one you'll be killing today. I suspect it will be more like yourself, for failing yet again."

She gestured at me with her chin as she spoke those words. On instinct, I glanced down at myself. My blood turned to ice, and I felt faint at the sight of the pink glow around my hand. I jerked my arm up to have a closer look at my ring. It was indeed glowing pink.

Astrid had opened the Sealed Door.

Traxia burst out laughing, her face and voice dripping with contempt. "You fool. I'm the daughter of a Royal Sea Witch and blood bound to the kraken. Even with you keeping me trapped in the dungeon, how could you possibly think I wasn't powerful enough to mess with her feeble mind and yours at the same time? Tick tock brother. Come see me take over your woman."

"NO!" I shouted, dashing for the door.

Before I finished running past her, the fake Astrid's face and exposed skin cracked then collapsed into a pile of ashes on the floor. I ignored it and ran as fast as my legs allowed. The whole way down to the dungeon, I shouted Astrid's name, praying to all the Gods that she wouldn't let Traxia in, wouldn't yield to her control.

In my haste, I tripped halfway down the stairs to the dungeon, tumbling down and rolling to a brutal stop at the bottom. From the sharp pain radiating in my left shoulder, I'd likely dislocated it. But that, too, I ignored.

"Astrid! Astrid, please! Don't do this," I begged, running the short distance to the open door. "Please, my love, please! I can't lose you. Not like this, not now. Come back to me, Astrid."

She was standing inside the room, Traxia's ominous silhouette filling the psyche behind her, an evil air of triumph on her face as she gazed possessively at my wife.

Astrid turned to look at me, her hair disheveled, her eyes dull, and the dark circles beneath them making her look broken and worn out.

Guilt and sorrow flitted over her features. "I'm sorry, Erik. I can't do this anymore. The Gods know I tried. I really tried. Please, forgive me."

"NOOOO!" I yelled, running towards the room as she turned and extended a hand towards the mirror.

I entered the room, just as Traxia's slender fingers with long, pointy nails, extruded out of the psyche and closed over Astrid's wrist. My wife cried out, and I fell to my knees, crushed, as Traxia's essence flowed out of the psyche and into Astrid's body.

Her evil laughter echoed throughout the room.

"I win, little brother. I *always* win. Now, what are you going to do? Will you kill your wife, or kill yourself?"

CHAPTER 12
ASTRID

A splitting headache had needles stabbing at the back of my eyes. Traxia was everywhere, her siren's song more potent... more vicious than ever. Erik should have helped dampen her voice by now. He should have distracted me with his own voice like he had done so many times before. But not tonight, not this time.

Something is wrong.

Erik was always attentive to me the minute the sun went down, ready to refocus my attention away from Traxia as soon as she began her attack. But my husband was nowhere to be found.

As usual, we had an early supper so that the servants could leave before nightfall. After our meal, Erik had excused himself to go handle some papers he needed to have ready first thing in the morning. He had claimed it would be no more than thirty minutes, then he'd join me in our bedroom. As we now spent most of our nights awake because of Traxia's constant assaults, we tried to get some sleep early, with naps during the day.

I got in bed with a book, the words increasingly blurring before my eyes as my tormentor's attack began, then gradually escalated.

Erik never returned.

When the clock marked the following hour, I knew something was seriously wrong. I got up on wobbly legs, my stomach roiling from the excruciating pain in my head. Traxia no longer bothered trying to lure me. She was merely trying to break me. No more enticing songs, no more pretty illusions, only banshee screeches and ear-splitting noises at maximum volume playing non-stop inside my head.

With drunken steps, I headed towards Erik's study. Traxia's rabid screeches grew louder with each step. Tears of pain welled in my eyes, and I called out Erik's name.

In vain.

By the time I reached his study, tears drenched my face. When I opened the door to find it empty, violent sobs rocked my body. I couldn't do this anymore. At this point, I'd do anything, give anything just for a moment of peace and quiet. Even death was better than this torture.

As I turned away from Erik's study, leaning heavily on the wall for support, the intensity of the cacophony in my head appeared to dampen. I couldn't say if it was real or just me adapting to this threshold of agony, but I welcomed it.

Moving as fast as my condition permitted, I hastened towards the music room. But a beloved voice amidst the screaming had me jerking my head left to look over my shoulder.

Erik! That was Erik!

I had heard his voice in my ears, not inside my head. Spinning on my heels, I shouted his name while running in the direction his voice came from. The loud screeches in my mind tripled in intensity. I cried out from the pain and fell to my knees. I heaved a couple of times, my stomach constricting horribly as I waited for my mind to fracture.

The sound of Erik's voice screaming my name again in horror had whipped me back into action. Forcing myself back up, I ran forward only to be brought down again by a lancing pain at the back of my head. It felt as if someone was taking an ax to my head.

I'm coming, Erik. I'm coming!

Half running, half crawling, I pushed forward in the direction his voice had emanated from only to realize they were coming from the dungeon, its massive doors standing wide open. Why would Erik be down in the dungeon, especially this late in the evening? Was I hallucinating? Was this another of Traxia's tricks to get me in front of the Sealed Door?

But what if he's truly down there and in distress?

The atrocious headache made it impossible for me to think straight.

"I WILL KILL YOU!" Erik's muffled voice shouted in the distance.

Oh, Gods! Who is he talking to? Who is he threatening? Who else is here?

With a surge of energy I didn't think I still possessed, I shot up to my feet and ran to the door. As I started running down the stairs, I opened my mouth to call out Erik again, but the words of his interlocutor silenced me and stopped me dead in my tracks.

"You can't kill me, you fool," Traxia said, her voice filled with contempt. "If I die, you will no longer be able to harness my power. You overplayed your hand, dear brother. You thought she was a skittish, easily manipulated little girl. But I believe she will actually beat you at your own game and complete your challenge. Then both the kraken and I will become *hers* to control. You may have fooled your aunt and that waste of oxygen she calls her new Royal Sea Witch, but you and I both know the truth. And your dear wife will expose you for the true monster you are."

Erik chuckled, the unusually high-pitched sound sending icy chills down my spine. I knew that laughter. It had haunted me a million times while Traxia taunted me. Surely, he hadn't pretended to be...?

"Oh, Traxia. After all these years, I would have thought you would have learned a thing or two," Erik said smugly with a cruelty and malice that made my gorge rise. "I haven't needed your help to control the kraken in a very long time. Who do you think unleashed it against my parents?"

"You?!" Traxia exclaimed, her voice filled with horror and disbelief. "But how? He's bound to *me*! That's why everyone accused *me*!"

Erik laughed again. "We're siblings, remember? Your blood bond with the kraken also bound it to me. You mock Inga and Aunt Eira, and yet they knew of my bond with the beast."

"They knew?! No. There's no way Eira would support you if she knew you killed her brother," Traxia exclaimed.

I felt faint. None of this could be true. Leaning against the wall for support, I took a few steps down to see what was happening down there. I felt my blood drain from my face at the spectacle before me.

For a split second, I thought Erik had opened the door, but then realized it had either gone transparent, or a secondary glass door kept his sister trapped within. The room appeared to be filled with water, Traxia—a true mermaid—floating in front of her brother. Her blonde hair—the same color as their late father's mane—danced around her face like a golden halo. Her tail, with long flowy fins was the same pale color as her hair with little specks of gold.

How can someone so beautiful be this evil?

But then, was she? If any of this conversation was true, then Erik had been the monster all along.

"They do not know. To them, I only found out a few weeks ago that I have sway over the kraken," Erik said mockingly. "They think me madly in love with that bore I call a wife. I played along for them to give me tricks on breaking *your* hold over Astrid. I couldn't allow you to further poison her mind against me."

"Astrid only has to last two more months. Then you will be stuck with her forever, *and* you will have lost *me*," Traxia hissed. "Once this room is fully sealed—"

"Once this room is fully sealed, you will both have served your purpose," Erik interrupted with disdain. "There's a reason I only performed a handfasting. Once the year is up, either party can decide to end the union. I will send her back to her father. Anyway, each seal she activates leeches away her life force. If the final one doesn't kill her, it will leave her but a shadow of herself."

"That fool loves you!" Traxia exclaimed.

Erik waved a dismissive hand. "Love is an illusion. Give a female a few orgasms, and she'll be ready to kill for you. Astrid loves my cock, like your mother loved my father's."

"YOU BASTARD!" Traxia hissed.

Erik chuckled. "Actually, *you* are the bastard. I'm legitimate. But take heart, your misery will soon end. My ring doesn't just warn me of my current wife possibly giving in to temptation. Where Astrid's medallion leeches out her life force to charge the seals, the ring will absorb all the energy and power contained within this room. Once Astrid completes the challenge, all her energy and the one my previous wives fed the door, *and* all *your* power and magic will be transferred to me. You will die, but I'm sure you will prefer death to eternity trapped in this dark room."

"Or your wife, who has proven stronger than anyone expected, can discover your ploy, get rid of the necklace, and expose you for who you really are," Traxia said.

Her silver eyes flicked up to look straight at me. My breath caught in my throat, and my blood turned to ice when Erik abruptly turned his head to look over his shoulder at what his sister was staring at.

Shock, anger, and disbelief crossed his features in quick succession, before settling on an almost sad expression.

"Astrid, Astrid, Astrid… You had been doing so well. Never

sticking your nose where it didn't belong. Showing exceptional resistance to temptation. But you had to come and spy on me now. I'm very disappointed," Erik said with resignation.

"RUN, ASTRID! Remove that necklace and run!" Traxia shouted.

"No, dear wife," Erik said in a menacing tone. The pitch change and the vibration in his voice struck me like a hammer. "Come to me, Astrid."

With a will of their own, my legs forced me down the stairs towards him, when every fiber of my being screamed for me to run away. As I made my way down the stairs, enthralled by his compulsion, Erik casually turned back to face his sister.

"Enough out of you for tonight."

With these words, he pulled out his ring from the deeper recess inside the keyhole where I normally placed my nautilus medallion to charge the seals. A magical glow spread over the glass, which darkened before returning to its thick wooden appearance.

Erik turned back to look at me. He shook his head in a way that appeared to mean 'What a waste' as he pulled out an ornate dagger from his belt.

"Erik, what are you going to do?" I asked in a breathy, terrified voice.

"What you forced me to do, Astrid. I really wanted to set you free after this was all done. But you had to meddle in my affairs," Erik said matter-of-factly. "Do not fret. I will make it swift."

With all my might, I tried to fight his compulsion. For a moment, I felt myself regain a sliver of control over my legs.

"Do not resist. Come to me," Erik repeated more forcefully, his voice making it impossible for me not to comply.

This had to be an illusion. This couldn't be real. He couldn't have so completely fooled me for ten months. I had shared this man's bed. He had held me and comforted me through the difficult times of this ordeal. All the times he professed his love for me, the sincerity in his eyes and his voice had been undeniable. This couldn't be real.

In a flash of lucidity, I realized the dreadful pain that had been wrecking my brain had stopped a while back. In fact, it had stopped when I'd started listening in on their conversation. That was too convenient. Even as my feet led me mercilessly towards my death, I pulled a pin in my hair. Confusion and disbelief settled over Erik's handsome face. He probably thought I intended to use it as a weapon to fight him.

I would never stand a chance against him.

Instead, I stabbed the back of my hand with it. I hissed at the pain—true pain, not the dull one I usually felt when trapped in an illusion. For a brief moment, choking terror crushed me. If I felt real pain, then I was truly standing in the dungeon, a short distance away from Erik, about to get killed by the man I'd given my heart and soul to.

And then his image flickered.

Although I stopped walking forward, I was still rooted in place. Erik's appeared to melt before me like a life-size wax statue. Simultaneously, the muffled sound of a voice pierced through the fog. My vision cleared only to reveal that I was in fact standing directly in front of the closed Sealed Door, Erik on his knees at my feet. His face drenched in tears, he looked completely crushed... devastated.

"Go on, Erik! Kill me or kill yourself! You lost!"

I nearly jumped out of my skin upon hearing such heinous words spat angrily at Erik in my voice. The voice had come from behind me. But to Erik, it would sound as if I had spoken them. A single glance at his face and at the glazed look of his eyes convinced me he was hallucinating.

Horror washed over me as I finally understood what Machiavellian plan she had set for us. If Erik killed me or killed himself, she would win. Traxia realized she would never get me to turn the key clockwise. If she couldn't make me give in to temptation, she would just kill me.

"ERIK! WAKE UP!" I shouted, throwing myself at him.

With an enraged cry, he immediately tried to subdue me. I didn't fight. My husband was far too strong, more than a normal human. Instead, I stabbed my hair pin into his forearm.

He grunted in pain then seized my wrist. Before he could push me away or pin me down, I wrapped my free arm around his neck and pressed myself to him, my cheek against his.

"You didn't fail, Erik. *I* didn't fail. The door is still closed. This is an illusion. Feel the pain in your arm and look at the door. It is closed! The medallion is still around my neck."

My heart skipped a beat when he tore me away from him and pulled out the dagger from his belt.

"It's me, Erik. Look at my chest. Look at your ring. The door is still sealed," I pleaded with a weepy voice, while tears welled in my eyes. "Please, my love. We've come so far. Come back to me."

Erik blinked, his eyes appearing to go out of focus before locking with the medallion hanging around my neck. Shock, disbelief, and confusion warred over his features. He jerked his head up to look at the door behind me, the oddest mix of horror and relief settling on his face.

"Astrid?" he asked, looking at me as if he couldn't believe I was real.

"Yes, Erik. It's me," I said with a teary laugh.

"Oh, Gods! Astrid!" he exclaimed, tossing his dagger as if it was burning his hand.

He pulled me into a bruising embrace even as he jumped to his feet. Holding me in his arms, he ran out of the dungeon, climbing each step two at a time, as if an army of demons was hot on our trail. I hung on to him, laughing and crying at the same time. Traxia's enraged voice in my head cussing us out made me laugh harder.

Once back in our bedroom, he put me down on my feet, letting go of me only long enough to close the door. He immediately went back to touching me, the way a parent would to make sure their child hadn't sustained any injury after a serious fall.

"I'm fine, Erik. Everything is fine. I promise," I said, still laughing even as tears trickled down my cheeks.

"I thought I lost you," he said in a tortured voice. "You had opened the door and surrendered—"

"NEVER! I will *never* surrender to her, and she knows it," I said forcefully, interrupting him. "Traxia is growing desperate. If she can't sway me, then she will try to eliminate one of us. As long as you and I continue to look after each other, she can't win. I love you, Erik. I'm not going anywhere."

"My beautiful wife, you are everything to me," Erik said fervently before crushing my lips in an almost desperate kiss.

I melted against him, his love wrapping around me like a warm blanket on a cold winter night. Latching on to this feeling, I filed it away deep within. Every time Traxia made me doubt, I would recall this moment and the sincerity of his love.

He broke the kiss and rested his forehead against mine in a moment of tenderness.

"What happened?" I asked in a soft voice after a beat.

Erik closed his eyes and groaned angrily. "I let my guard down for too long," he said. "I let her get the best of me."

"No, Erik. She got the upper hand for a short while, but in the end you prevailed," I corrected.

"*We* prevailed, mostly thanks to you," he said, clearly still mad at himself.

"We prevailed because *you* gave me the tools necessary to pull my own weight. Your love is what keeps me going, Erik. Without you and the endless support you've given me, I would have failed a long time ago."

He smiled gratefully, then lured me to the couch. I settled in his lap and snuggled against him in the way I loved so much. A soft purr rose from my throat when he gently caressed my back, making him chuckle.

He sighed, sobering, then launched into a retelling of what had happened. I lifted my head to look at him when he hesitated about describing what had occurred in the gallery.

"Let me guess, the portraits were telling me to get rid of the necklace, run away, and tell everyone that you're the real monster," I said, matter-of-factly.

Erik blanched, his eyes flicking between mine to assess my thoughts. I smiled and caressed his beard.

"Traxia has used that one on me a few times. I don't believe it. You've proven to me time and again that you love me," I said with conviction. "Her only chance of winning is breaking us up, turning us against each other. That will never happen. Every time she tries to paint you as a monster, she loses her hold over me."

"I am glad to hear it. The horrors she says about me..." Erik said with a haunted look.

"You have no idea," I replied, a shiver running down my spine as I explained to him about the illusion she had created of him being a power-hungry monster, who'd gone so far as to kill his parents to ascend the throne sooner.

Hatred burned in his eyes as I spoke those words.

"Is nothing too low for her?" he hissed.

"Apparently not. And this is why you cannot allow yourself to be this vulnerable again," I said cautiously.

Erik stiffened and looked at me questioningly. I shifted in his lap and tucked a lock of hair behind my ear while carefully choosing my words.

"You used to be immune to her siren song," I explained. "Before, I had to tell you that she was talking to me for you to know. Now, you immediately sense it and create a distraction."

"Yes, it's to protect you," he said, clearly taken aback that I should challenge his actions. "The sooner I intervene, the less you suffer."

"But the more you listen for her, and the more vulnerable you become," I gently argued. "I need you to keep me grounded. You can't do that if you're battling for your own sanity. Shield yourself. I will tell you as soon as she starts acting up. And if she has me too far gone, hurt me."

Erik recoiled. "WHAT?!"

I nodded forcefully. "You heard me right. There's a reason I stabbed you with my hair pin. By the way, sorry about that. But real physical pain helps break the illusion. I guess it's our survival instincts forcing us to take a proper look at our surroundings. Getting physically hurt in her illusions does not feel the same as in reality. Pinch me or something and tell me to feel the pain."

His eyes flicked from side to side as if trying to remember something, then he refocused on me with an air of wonder. "You're right. I fell down the stairs and thought I had dislocated my shoulder. But now I can see the pain was off. By the Gods, you never cease to amaze me," he whispered.

I shrugged and gave him a smug smile. "You are stuck with me, King Erik Thorsen. There are no limits to how creative I will get to beat this curse. But right now, I want to get creative in a very different way, dear husband."

Erik's eyes widened before smoldering. My cheeks heated at my boldness. Usually, my husband initiated and took control of our intimacy. While I was more than happy to yield to his dominance, I sometimes wanted to take the lead. He was so stunning, his body such perfection. Seeing him shiver under my touch, moan in response to my caresses, and fall apart for me always made me feel like a goddess.

I leaned forward, my lips brushing over his as my hands roamed over his muscular abdominal muscles. He leaned into the kiss, instinctively trying to take over. I pulled away and gave him the same type of stern look he often gave me when he wanted me submissive.

"Tut, tut! It's your Queen's turn now to have her way with you," I said in a severe tone laced with sensuality. "I want to do naughty things to you."

"By all means, my Queen. I am yours to do with as you please," he replied in a rumbling voice, his silver eyes darkening like a stormy sky.

With a triumphant smile, I reclaimed his lips, my hands slipping under the soft fabric of his shirt. Even as our tongues mingled, I rubbed my palms over the chiseled grooves of his stomach, gliding his shirt up as they journeyed towards his chest. By the Gods, how I loved the feel of his smooth skin, and the hardened nubs of his nipples beneath my touch.

I interrupted the kiss only long enough to remove his shirt. The taste of the red wine we'd had earlier during our meal lingered on his breath, making me even more drunk with desire for my man. Fisting his shoulder-length midnight-blue hair at the nape, I gently but firmly pulled his head back.

The sound of his sharp breath resonated directly between my thighs as I let my lips explore his face. The silky strands of his beard tickled them as they journeyed down to his neck. Sticking my tongue out, I licked the barely visible lines that marked what he had told me turned into gills once he dove into salt water. Without him telling me, I never would have known and simply assumed they were old, mostly faded scars. I hated that I couldn't go to the ocean with him to bear witness to this other side of him. But soon... very soon, I would.

He shivered, his fingers slipping through my hair to settle on my nape. To my delight, he didn't try to control me, letting me explore his body as I saw fit. I sucked on his closed gills a few moments longer before slipping off his lap as I continued down to his chest. Pushing his legs apart, I kneeled between them, my hands still caressing his stomach while my tongue teased his nipples.

Erik moaned again, his abdominal muscles quivering

between my touch. I smiled once more even as I closed my lips around his little nub, slowly sucking on it. I flicked my thumb at the other one before tweaking it, not hard enough to hurt, but sufficiently to give it a nice sting. His grunt of approval emboldened me. My man loved a bit of pain.

While continuing to lick and nip at his nipple, I unfastened his breeches and freed my prize. Erik hissed, his back straightening when my hand closed around his length—or at least tried to. His thick girth made it impossible for my fingers to touch around it. Pressing my free palm to his chest, I pushed him back against the backrest of the settee while giving him a stern look.

Eyes locked with his, I reveled in my power over him as he stared back at me with hooded eyes and parted lips. His breathing grew louder as I began to stroke him. Gods, how I loved the look on his face and the way he reacted to the pleasure I was giving him. However, as much as I wanted to continue feasting my eyes on his beauty, my mouth was watering for a taste of him.

I kissed a path down his stomach, his increasingly labored breathing spurring me on. The strangled way he cried out my name when I closed my lips around the tip of his cock had moisture pooling between my thighs. I was supposed to be pleasuring him, and yet his moans in my ears and the silky texture of his member on my tongue had my inner walls constricting with need.

I bobbed over him, my hand moving in counterpoint to the movement of my mouth. Soon, his rapturous moans, the way his hand fisted in my hair, and the involuntary spasms in his legs warned me of his imminent climax. I accelerated the pace, grazing his length with my teeth on each upward motion, and teasing him with my tongue as I took him deep in my throat.

Erik suddenly emitted a savage grunt. For a split second, I thought he had found his release. But I yelped instead when he yanked my head back away from him. Before I realized what was happening, he leaned forward, grabbed my waist, and threw me backward with herculean strength. I flew through the air, my shocked scream fading into a startled gasp when I landed on the softness of our mattress.

Dazed and confused, I gaped at my husband only to see him stepping out of his breeches, which had fallen around his ankles. My stomach did a couple of backflips in both fear and arousal when he lunged at me with an almost feral look on his face. I thought Erik would jump on top of me and ram himself in before unleashing his passion on me. Instead, he grabbed the hem of my nightgown, tearing it open as if it had been a vulgar sheet of parchment.

This time, my gasp turned into a needy voluptuous moan when Erik buried his face between my thighs. He didn't launch into his usual slow foreplay or tease me with the most exquisite torture as was usually his wont. His lips immediately latched onto my little nub, sucking it with a frenzy while two of his fingers sank deep inside me.

My back arched off the bed as pleasure swiftly built in fiery waves within me. Erik's expert fingers making love to me kept grazing the sensitive spot inside me with deadly accuracy, sending lightning sparks throughout my body. I gave myself over to him, one hand settling on the back of his head while I fondled my breast with the other. Legs trembling with my imminent climax, I chanted his name, spurring him on as he continued to touch me exactly the way I needed.

My orgasm struck me with sweeping violence. I cried out, my body shaking as my spirit soared. Erik didn't stop feasting on me for a while longer as I continued to fly high. It was only once I started coming back down that he finally relented. To my surprise, he didn't immediately climb on top of me. Instead, he took a moment to rid me of the remaining tatters of my nightgown.

A deep moan rolled out of my throat when he finally lay

down on me, the searing heat of his bare skin wrapped all around mine.

"Do you have any idea how much I love you?" he whispered in an almost tortured voice while looking at me with adoration.

My tears pricked from the powerful emotion that surged within me. But Erik didn't give me a chance to respond, his lips claiming mine with a passion laced with tenderness that made me melt from the inside out. Even as our tongues mingled, Erik started pushing himself inside me. By the Gods, how I loved this man.

The way he looked at me, touched me, talked to me, I never thought anyone could ever make me feel this desirable or cherished. I didn't have that delicate-boned, slender figured, and porcelain skinned aesthetic that was deemed the summum of beauty in Rathlin.

Compared to women like Hilda or my sister, I always felt lacking with my thick bones, generous curves, naturally tanned skin, further darkened by my propensity to walk outside without an umbrella to shelter from the sun. But Erik made me feel like the embodiment of perfection, proven time and time again by the burning desire that always burned in his eyes when he gazed upon me, and the rabid hunger with which he claimed me, body and soul.

The initial burn of his possession quickly faded. Our voices mingled in blissful sighs as he gradually picked up the pace. My nails dug into his back as I lifted my pelvis to meet him thrust for thrust. Liquid fire ran through my veins while a pool of lava swirled in the pit of my stomach. My skin tingled as wave upon wave of ecstasy washed over me. I was drowning in an ocean of pleasure. The sound of flesh meeting flesh, my voluptuous moans, and Erik's labored breath interspersed with sinful words filled my ears.

My spine seized, and a blinding light flashed before my eyes as my orgasm crashed into me. I cried out, my body trembling in my husband's arms. Erik shouted as my inner walls clamped down on his length. But he didn't relent. Something seemed to break inside him, and he finally unleashed the beast.

His hands tightened on me in a bruising hold as he pounded into me with reckless abandon. Teeth clenched, eyes closed as if from excruciating pain, Erik was emitting almost feral grunts between moans. I felt on the verge of combusting from the inferno raging inside of me. I thought I would break from his brutal possession, swallowing me into a maelstrom of pleasure and pain. And yet I didn't want him to stop, even if my mind fractured from the excess of sensations.

I never saw the next orgasm coming. For a moment I felt as if my consciousness had been knocked out of my body. My mouth opened in a silent O while Erik threw his head back and roared his own release. His movements became erratic as he continued to pump in and out of me, his seed erupting inside me in powerful spurts. My head rolling from side to side on the mattress, I flew high on the wings of ecstasy until the room finally stopped spinning around me.

Utterly destroyed, I let Erik gather me in his embrace as he rolled onto his back. Head resting on his chest, I fell asleep to the thundering sound of his heart slowly settling down, and the words of love my husband whispered in my ears.

CHAPTER 13
ASTRID

From that fateful day forward, the bond between Erik and me grew even stronger. However, that didn't stop our evenings from becoming real nightmares. Traxia's voice had grown in urgency and potency. She was running out of time with only the nights to break me—to break *us*. She had redoubled her efforts in attempting to drive Erik insane. Thankfully, with his defenses back up, she wasn't getting anywhere with him.

My husband was my hero. He never left my side, putting the affairs of running the realm second to my needs. Whenever I couldn't sleep, Erik would stay awake from dusk until dawn to keep me distracted from her enticements. Despite that, some nights would get so difficult, I thought I'd go insane.

In my despair, I had asked him to cage me or chain me. Of course, that would have been too easy. As part of the curse, I couldn't be held against my will or physically prevented from opening the Sealed Door, if it was my desire. All Erik could do was try to sway me until I granted unequivocal consent for him to take me elsewhere. Only then could he carry me away.

On the plus side, it turned out that Traxia wasn't much of a voyeur. Whenever Erik and I would become intimate—well beyond a mere kiss or some light petting—Traxia's harassing voice would fade away. I doubted bashfulness or reluctance to spy on her brother playing naughty had anything to do with it. Each time I experienced intense moments of happiness or plea-sure, she retreated. That led me to suspect that she needed misery to thrive and latch on to.

Surprisingly, the strength and intensity of her assaults suddenly diminished. It unnerved us. Was her power weakening, or was she gathering her strength for one ultimate, devastating attack? As speculating got us nowhere, we decided to enjoy this partial reprieve while remaining on our guard.

Thus we chipped away at the remaining weeks of my chal-lenge. December came and went, followed by a snowy, chilly January. It was my birthday this month, and Erik organized a ball in my honor. Excitement bubbled through me as the elite of Rathlin walked into the ballroom. Standing by my husband's side on the balcony overlooking the room, I got an eerie déjà vu of my first time in this room.

"I was standing right here, eleven months ago, depressed at the thought of choosing another wife. The whole time, I had to listen to Hilda brag about how she was certain I'd choose her," Erik said wistfully.

"So you *were* here!" I exclaimed. "I thought there was someone watching us. But when I looked up, the balcony was too dark to see anything."

He smiled, the tenderness in his eyes making me melt from the inside out. With the back of two fingers, he caressed my cheeks and then my lips.

"Yes, I was. I always stand here to get an idea of what people are really like when they think I'm not around," Erik said with a sliver of disdain in his voice. "I felt quite distraught looking at those maidens. None of them were queen material, and much less strong enough to face this challenge. I was going to ask Tormund to just pick the one whose family needed the bride token the most when I finally saw you. You took my breath away."

"What?" I asked, stunned by his words. "But why? I was so incredibly awkward that night. With my family on the verge of being destitute, the others didn't want to associate with me. I kept telling myself it had been a mistake to come. If the other maidens, some of lower status than me, deemed me unworthy, why would our king even spare me a glance?"

"And yet, you were the most beautiful and the most graceful of them all," he countered with a fervor that had goosebumps erupting all over me. "I wanted you the moment I laid eyes on you. When I asked Tormund about you, and he told me of your family's financial troubles, it felt like fate. And the moment we danced, I knew you were the one."

Another delicious shiver ran down my spine at the way his voice dipped as he pronounced that last sentence. Slipping an arm around my waist, he drew me against his firm body. I melted into him.

"The way you felt in my embrace, you set my blood on fire. There was an innocence to you, laced with a boldness and strength that I found incredibly enticing. And yet, I almost let you go," Erik said, sounding like he couldn't believe it.

"Why? Because of Hilda?" I asked, curious.

"Absolutely not. I can't stand her," Erik said with disgust. "I wished for you to want me, like I wanted you. I hated that you were just considering marrying me because of what I could do for your family. But above all, I wanted you to live. I didn't think that..."

I smiled and caressed his hair when his voice trailed off. "You didn't think I would last."

His brow creased. "I prayed you would, but I'd been disappointed so many times."

"And instead, here you are, breaking your own rule by

holding a formal event involving your queen before the curse has been lifted," I said teasingly.

Erik snorted, his arms tightening around me as he gave me an unrepentant smile. "Since you're not allowed to fail, there's no reason for me not to properly celebrate my queen's birthday. Speaking of which, we should go mingle with our guests."

I nodded, reveling in the tender kiss he gave me before leading me down to the ground floor.

It was odd finding myself in the ballroom again amidst a crowd. This time, instead of being the pariah trying to make herself invisible among a smattering of hopeful maidens, I was the center of attention. The blatant ogling, speculating gazes and assessing stares quickly grated on my already frayed nerves.

Traxia's voice had stirred again moments before the first guests had begun arriving. It was relentless. A part of me would have given anything to simply curl up in Erik's arms while awaiting the blessed sunrise so that I might escape the castle again. But I intended to fully enjoy myself tonight. Hopefully, it would drive my tormentor away.

At first, I worried about having so many strangers in the castle after nightfall. But Erik reassured me that a single evening, with this many people, wouldn't be a problem. Anyway, we wouldn't celebrate too late into the night. Thankfully, mingling with others in this wondrous glimpse of normalcy again indeed dampened Traxia's never-ending harassment.

As expected, my father didn't allow Kara to attend the ball. He believed he was protecting her—and himself—from my inevitable death. However, through the correspondence my sister and I regularly exchanged, he subtly kept himself apprised of my continued welfare. I couldn't wait for the next six weeks to be over so I could show him it had all been worth it, in more ways than one.

He would love Erik.

Unfortunately, everything wasn't just merriment and play in

these types of events. Lady Freya was droning on about the endless virtues of her oldest daughter Solveig. She hoped I would make her one of my ladies-in-waiting once the trial ended. Lady Freya was but the latest hopeful mother talking my ears off in a never-ending series of such opportunistic conversations.

My eyes sought Erik among the guests, hoping for a rescue. He was speaking with one of his councilors and frowned when he noticed my distraught expression. Guilt surged through me when I watched him trying to free himself to come to me. Shaking my head at him, I smiled in a way I hoped he'd find reassuring.

With a barely repressed sigh of aggravation, I interrupted the constant flow from Lady Freya's nearly non-existent lips with a vague excuse. Her already protuberant eyes bulging and her chubby hand clutching at her ample bosom in shock should have been comical. However, an increasingly pounding headache tore at me, putting me in a less than humorous disposition. My annoyance with my ambitious guests had brought back Traxia's assault with a vengeance.

I took refuge on the balcony overlooking the garden. The late January evening offered pleasantly brisk weather. Without a coat, my hideout would only provide a brief reprieve, but I would take whatever I could. I inhaled the fresh, crisp air biting at my nose. The sound of the door opening behind me drew my attention. Turning around, I slightly recoiled at the sight of Hilda closing the door before approaching me. She held a beautifully embroidered shawl, which she extended to me. Stunned, I accepted the unexpected present and wrapped it around me. I nearly moaned at the welcomed warmth it provided.

"Thank you, Lady Hilda. I really needed that."

"My pleasure, your Highness," Hilda said, smiling.

Her sudden kindness baffled me. Everyone knew Hilda always believed she would be Erik's bride and the one to end the curse. When he chose me over her, the hurt and confusion she'd felt had been plain to see. I expected sourness and bitter resentment from her in the face of my apparent success—not this considerate gesture.

Eyeing her cautiously, I wondered what obscure plan brewed in her mind, and when she would strike.

"You must be wondering what I could want, seeking you out here, away from prying eyes and indiscreet ears?" Hilda asked, her eyes sparkling with amusement.

My cheeks heated, and I hoped she would attribute their sudden redness to the cool air. "I must confess that I do."

Hilda wrapped her own shawl tighter around her delicate shoulders and leaned against the stone railing of the balcony. "Against all odds, it appears that you will succeed where all others have failed. You're well aware that I was... upset that King Erik didn't choose me. It certainly was a considerable blow to my pride. But I guess it was also a much-needed lesson in humility, which took me quite a few months to digest and accept."

My lips parted in stupor at her unexpected candor. Unimpressed by my lack of decorum, I schooled my features and gave her a gracious smile.

"To be fair, Lady Hilda, we all thought he'd choose you. I was just as shocked as you no doubt were."

"I believe it. Although, if I'm honest, a part of me was relieved." She giggled prettily at my dubious expression. "I'm serious. Despite all my bravado, I wondered if I could survive the challenge that defeated so many others. Whatever flaws I possess, being suicidal isn't one of them."

I couldn't help but chuckle at the self-derisive expression on her face. "Ah yes, self-preservation... My father deplores my apparent lack of it."

Hilda seemed surprised by my answer. "Your father didn't approve of you attending the ball?" When I shook my head, she looked utterly taken aback. "In light of your previous circumstances, this was the best possible outcome for your family!"

I shrugged, acting more casually than I felt. "It was. However, Father believed we could have found a different solution that wouldn't have put my life in jeopardy. He would have preferred we became destitute and have all his children alive, rather than be wealthy and in mourning."

A strange look crossed her features, then Hilda turned to face the frozen garden. She rested her hands on the stone railing. "I envy you, you know?"

"What?" I also leaned against the railing while admiring Hilda's regal profile.

She looked every bit the queen she had longed to become.

"My parents wouldn't particularly care if I died, as long as the king chose me. They would have only wanted me to last as long as possible before I keeled over. Were you aware that your bride price increases for every month you survive?"

I shook my head in complete shock. "This is the first I hear of this."

She snorted. "Ariana's mother became extravagant in her spendings after her daughter's handfasting—each month more outrageous than the last. When my mother inquired about the source of this new wealth, she confessed. Ever since, my parents have dreamed of the same privilege for themselves."

My heart went out to her. I couldn't begin to imagine what it must be like to be nothing more than a means to enrich themselves to the people who should care about you the most.

The balcony door opened behind us, revealing a worried Erik. He cast a concerned glance at Hilda before turning questioning eyes to me.

"Is everything all right, my darling?" Erik asked, closing the distance between us.

"Everything is fine, Erik," I said, smiling. "Lady Hilda and I were having a friendly conversation. Were you looking for me?"

He blinked, no doubt trying to hide his surprise. "Yes, actually I was. It's time to open the ball."

I gave Hilda an apologetic smile. She curtsied gracefully as Erik led me inside. Finding myself in the arms of my beloved under the speculating gazes of countless strangers brought me back to my first night in the castle. This time, no nerves, worries, or desperate imaginings filled my mind as I whirled and twirled on the dance floor. All that mattered was the loving way in which my husband stared at me, as if I was the greatest wonder in the world. In that moment, everything that wasn't us ceased to exist.

The ball lasted for a couple of hours. Whenever possible, I danced with Erik, but otherwise accepted the requests of our guests, as a proper hostess should. On a few occasions, I caught myself looking for Hilda, but she was nowhere to be seen. Had she made a discreet exit while we were dancing? However, she suddenly reappeared when Erik publicly gave me my birthday presents.

Tears welled in my eyes when he pulled a drape to reveal a life-size portrait of me in a royal gown, playing Sora—my mother's harp. But when he presented me with the real instrument—which he had bought from my father—the dam broke. I didn't even care that I was making a spectacle of myself.

Whatever doubts anyone might have had about the genuine love between the king and me faded away. Even with nearly seven weeks left to go before, the dubious look our guests had cast on me upon their arrival had now given way to hope. They, too, believed I just might make it.

With the night coming to an end, the guests took turns bidding their goodnight to Erik and me, Hilda among them.

"Lady Hilda," I said, smiling when she came to pay her respect. "Thank you for coming."

"The pleasure was all mine, your Highness," Hilda said. She curtsied and turned as if to leave but changed her mind. "If I may be so bold, I rather enjoyed our conversation earlier. Would it be acceptable if I came back to visit now and then?"

I felt Erik's startled glance. The request was unexpected, but I, too, had enjoyed our conversation. I also missed the feminine companionship my sister and I used to share. Hilda no doubt had ulterior motives. But right now, I would settle for anything other than the servants' reluctant surveillance.

"It would be lovely to have you over for tea, Lady Hilda," I replied. "I'm always home, so feel free to come by whenever you please."

She seemed delighted by my answer. After a final curtsey, she took her leave.

~

M y head was throbbing from the strain of Traxia's constant and desperate assaults. With only four days away from March first, and the activation of the final seal, Traxia no longer kept her attacks to nighttime. Twice more, I had nearly given Erik a heart attack by sleepwalking to the door. Tricked each time in broad daylight by even more deceptive daydreams. Sleep deprivation was taking its toll on me. Even the hunters' pavilion was failing to provide any kind of real relief anymore.

I was preparing to go on a horseback ride to the edge of the estate when Tormund informed me Hilda had come calling. This was her eleventh visit since my birthday celebration six weeks ago. Our relationship remained somewhat awkward, but her company had become a welcomed distraction, especially to give Erik a slight reprieve to handle matters of the state. She was smart, worldly, and shared my passion for embroidery and poetry. As an accomplished flutist, Hilda played many duets with me while I played my mother's harp. Erik even surprised us by sitting in at one of our sessions.

"Hello, Lady Hilda," I said while putting on my riding

gloves. "I was just heading out for a ride. Would you care to join me?"

Under different circumstances, I would have postponed it, but I desperately needed to get out of the castle. Accommodating as ever, Hilda bowed her head in acknowledgment.

"It would be my pleasure, your Highness."

We rode for nearly an hour in the surrounding woodlands. As I needed to clear my head, I set a rather intense pace, not overly conducive to conversation. By the time we returned to the castle, I was chilled to the bone. Hilda didn't utter the slightest complaint at my inconsiderate behavior. While she tried hard to hide it, her shivering spoke volumes about her level of discomfort. Ashamed, I asked the servants to bring us tea in my boudoir.

I stood by the fireplace, my palms extended towards the flames to warm my frozen hands. Hilda sat behind me on a couch across the hearth. Minutes later, a servant came in with tea and biscuits, which she lay on the coffee table in front of Hilda. The soothing fragrance of herbal tea soon filled the room.

"Sugar and milk?" Hilda asked, pouring us tea.

"Yes, please. That would be lovely," I said over my shoulder.

After lingering a moment longer by the fire, I took a seat in front of Hilda, across from the coffee table. She presented me with a cup which I gratefully took from her. I couldn't repress the moan of pleasure that escaped me at the first sip, blessed warmth spreading through me. Hilda smiled then drank from her own cup with a contented sigh.

"You are proving quite gracious, Lady Hilda, despite my rather rude behavior," I said sheepishly. "It was far too cold for such a long ride. Yet, you have kept the pace without so much as a remonstrance for my callousness. Please accept my apologies."

Hilda shrugged. "No apologies needed, your Highness. You're clearly under a great deal of stress. I can see that your trial is taking its toll on you. It's my great honor to support you in whatever capacity I may."

"You're so kind and understanding. I've greatly enjoyed your companionship over the past few weeks. However, under the circumstances, I cannot help but wonder about your motives for this sudden display of friendship."

"Why indeed? Well, since you are asking so bluntly, I will be as forward with my answer." She took another sip of her tea, then set it down on the table and looked me straight in the eye. "As you well know, I wanted to be King Erik's queen. While it's now obvious that I will never be, my ambitions haven't dampened. In less than a week, you will be officially acknowledged as Queen of the Rathlin Islands. As such, you'll partake in many royal functions, which will put you in frequent contact with the most powerful men of our allied and neighboring kingdoms. Any woman smart enough to secure a place by your side as your confidante or lady-in-waiting will have many opportunities to catch their eye."

I chuckled, flabbergasted by her honesty, unable to decide if I was impressed or offended. "Your candor astounds me, Lady Hilda. Aren't you afraid that such forwardness would behoove me to cast you from my side?"

Hilda smiled and bowed her head in a conciliatory fashion. "It would be foolish and arrogant of me to presume to know how you will or won't react. But I think I know you enough now to believe you do not suffer flatterers and sycophants. You would want the truth, however unpleasant it may be." Hilda refilled my cup, then hers, and gave me a teasing smile. "That said, I must confess that your company has proven quite enjoyable for me, too. Trying to ingratiate myself to you hasn't actually been the hardship I feared it would be."

This time, I burst out laughing at her boldness. She smiled smugly while adding sugar and milk to my cup. While I wasn't overly ambitious myself, I could respect such a trait in others.

Hilda would probably never be a confidante, but she had been a pleasant companion. I didn't mind helping her in securing a rich and powerful husband.

We devoted the next fifteen minutes or so to some mild gossiping as Hilda got me up to date on the latest events in the realm, outside the confines of the castle. However, the sleep deprivation that had plagued me suddenly demanded its due as an intense wave of weariness washed over me. My eyelids seemed to weigh a ton, and my mind struggled to form coherent thoughts.

Noticing my abrupt change in disposition, Hilda rushed to my side, a concerned expression on her face.

"Your Highness, are you unwell? Should I call for assistance?"

"Ti–tired… So tired…" I barely managed to say.

"Of course." Hilda sounded relieved. "With your current ordeal, you would be. Don't fight it, your Highness. Please lie down and rest awhile. All will be fine. I will stay by your side."

Hilda coaxed me into resting my head on the arm of the settee and put my feet up so I would lie down. I wanted to protest, but my mind was too foggy to even form words. Hilda fetched a throw blanket, which she laid atop me, still whispering comforting words. My last thought before darkness claimed me was how odd that Traxia's voice had gone silent.

CHAPTER 14
ASTRID

An acute chest pain and the impression of suffocating brought me out of my slumber. It was as if ice-cold hands dug sharp claws into my heart and choked my neck in a bruising hold. Clutching at my chest, I gasped for breath. I scrambled off the couch on unsteady feet and noticed Hilda's absence. She had promised to watch over me!

Though my gut knew better, I told myself she probably only stepped out for a few seconds. My weariness, however, had been too sudden, too brutal to have been natural. Then the ugly truth dawned on me. This chest pain and shortness of breath were familiar. I had felt the same when the medallion had warned me I was too far from the castle for too long. I looked down at my chest, already knowing my necklace would be gone.

"No! Hilda, you fool!" I breathed out.

Taking support on the furniture, I stumbled my way to the door of my boudoir. When I opened it, it was as if I had walked into Hell itself. Traxia's voice exploded in my head, shrieking for me to come to her at once. I cried out and doubled over in pain from the excruciatingly loud sound. On instinct, in a futile attempt to block her out, I slapped my hands over my ears.

"Your Highness, are you unwell?" a servant asked.

Overwhelmed by pain and fear, I barely registered her presence, too focused on blocking out Traxia and getting to Hilda before she did something irreversible. Supporting myself against the wall, I teetered towards the dungeon, shouting incoherently for Hilda to stop.

"Your Highness, please," the servant pleaded. "You mustn't go there! Please return to your boudoir, and I will ask Master Tormund to come see you."

Ignoring her, I plowed forward. She grabbed my arm to stop me. Shoving her more forcefully than I would have, had my mind not been so tortured by agony, I made a last dash for the dungeon's door and all but tore it open.

Traxia's vicious shouts inside my head drowned the fading voice of the servant shouting for Tormund to come at once. Lurching down the stairs, I almost fell more than once. When I reached the landing, I saw my greatest fear had come true. At the end of the corridor, past the octagonal hall, the eleven active seals pulsated red around the gaping darkness of the opened door.

Taking a few more steps forward, I halted in the middle of the octagon and peered inside the dark room ahead, afraid that I wouldn't be able to stop if I went any closer. Hilda stood in front of a magnificent psyche with a frame made of corals inlaid with precious gems. The soft purple glow from the corals was the only source of light in the formerly sealed room. Trapped inside the psyche, the beautifully cruel-looking Traxia sneered at me. How had I not seen her resemblance to Erik during our first encounter?

"Lost something, Queen Astrid?" the dual voices of Hilda and Traxia simultaneously said, while Hilda dangled the medallion from her uplifted hand. "You should come and get it. After that, everything will be fine. No more pain... No more fear... Just peace..."

The shrieking in my head had stopped. I knew I couldn't... shouldn't... Erik made me swear never to open the door or enter the room of my own free will. But I needed that necklace. I couldn't breathe. And that voice... That sweet, sweet, and beckoning voice... So tempting... So mesmerizing.

"Astrid," the dual voices commanded, "come to me..."

And I obeyed.

CHAPTER 15
ERIK

Four days... Only four more days and the nightmare that had ruined my life for the past fifteen years would be over. When I had chosen Astrid a year ago, I only expected to enjoy the company of a golden goddess for a few weeks or months until my half-sister claimed her life. And in exchange for her sacrifice, I would set her family with a prosperous future instead of the grim one that awaited them.

But I'd gotten so much more.

I never expected to fall in love with any of my brides. It wasn't until the first time Astrid almost opened the Sealed Door eight months ago that I realized the depth of my feelings for her. The thought of losing her *then* had been unbearable. The thought of losing her *now* was unfathomable.

Astrid was such a strong woman. Even with my defenses up, I could still hear the enticing siren song of my sister's summons. For having been subjected to its compulsion, I perfectly understood the power it wielded over its victims. Had I not been a hybrid, able to shield myself from Traxia, I would have lost my mind ages ago. That Astrid had withstood it all for so long only heightened my love and admiration for her.

I hated leaving my wife alone in the castle. However, with the trial ending in just a few days, I wanted to prepare a memorable surprise to show her she was my everything. I wanted the entire world to know there would never be another for me.

The unusually warm late winter sun was streaking through the stained-glass windows in Father Osvald's office at the back of the church. We were ironing out the last details of the sumptuous wedding I was planning for Astrid and me. It would take place on the last day of our handfasting, exactly one year and one day after we first met.

She had so badly wanted her father to give her away at the altar. Getting the stubborn old man to silence his fearful reluctance and commit to participate in the event had been quite the challenge. He believed that taking Astrid's success for granted was inviting fate to punish us for our arrogance by dooming her instead. However, I believed in the power of positive thinking while also taking every necessary measure to help destiny along the way.

Having wrapped our business, Father Osvald and I rose from our chairs and headed for the door.

"Mistress Brynhild is putting the final touches to a wedding gown for Queen Astrid," Father Osvald said. He opened his office door and gestured for me to go through first. "She's quite offended that you asked Tora to design it. She claims it is her greatest masterpiece and simply insists that you look at it before making your final decision as to who should dress the Queen."

I snorted at the seamstress' boast. Mistress Brynhild was without a doubt one of the most talented seamstresses of the realm—and the least humble. While I didn't doubt she had made a breathtaking gown, she had been among those who had turned their backs on Astrid and her family when they had fallen on hard times. Tora had remained steadfast, thus earning my wife's loyalty. Anyway, Kara had been working closely with Tora, making sure the design would be in line with Astrid's tastes.

"There's no question Mistress Brynhild has outdone herself. However, so did Tora, who also happens to know my wife's measurements perfectly as she never shunned her."

Father Osvald slowly nodded in understanding. He didn't need me to go into further details about how uncharitable people had been.

"But enough of such talks. Now is the time for rejoicing. It has been too long since we celebrated a royal wedding here," I said, my throat somewhat choked at the memory of the fourteen painful years prior to Astrid entering my life.

"It has," Father Osvald concurred.

We reached the entrance of the church and stopped by the open door. Father Osvald placed a comforting hand on my shoulder. "Your trial is over, my son. I couldn't have wished a better queen for you."

"Thank you, Father." I gave him my hand. "I couldn't have hoped for a more amazing woman."

When Father Osvald took my hand and shook it, my ring suddenly began to pulsate a bright, pinkish red.

"No…" I breathed, my heart seizing in my chest.

"Your Highness?" Father Osvald said, his eyes searching my face.

I yanked my hand from his grip and stared at the ring, hoping against hope that it was just a malfunction… that it would return to its safe whitish opalescent color. But I already knew…

"Astrid… no… Oh, dear Gods, no!" I ran blindly to my horse, my heart shattering to pieces. I couldn't breathe from the pain.

"Erik!" Father Osvald shouted behind me.

Ignoring him, I jumped onto Thunder's back and rode him hard to the castle, my eyes constantly darting back to the ring. Its current light hue meant one of two things: Astrid had either parted from the necklace, or she had opened the Sealed Door.

Traxia hadn't taken possession of Astrid yet. Once she initiated it, the gem would lose its pinkish hue and take on a pure red color that would darken over time until it turned black. Once that occurred, Traxia would freely walk in a new body, wreaking havoc and destruction. Whether Astrid had opened the door or parted from the necklace, there was still a chance to save her—as long as she didn't surrender to Traxia. The minute the gem turned red, and possession began, she would be forever lost to me. Traxia's presence would grow until she had completely taken over her victim. The only way to end the threat was to behead the host.

I couldn't... Not Astrid... She had to hang on.

The five-mile ride to the castle never felt so long. Halfway through, Thunder was lathered with sweat and frothing at the mouth. The poor beast was breathing so hard it sounded like roaring from where I was sitting. At this pace, if my mount didn't die along the way, he might never be the same, assuming he ever recovered. However, slowing down wasn't an option.

With less than a mile left to go, blood started seeping into the froth as my horse's lungs bled from the excessive exertion. The gem on my ring was still pinkish. My prayers alternated between Astrid not faltering and my horse's heart not giving out. The castle loomed in the distance when Thunder seriously began flagging. It was only a matter of minutes before he suffered a catastrophic failure. My horse staggered, its gait becoming sluggish and uncoordinated.

A couple of guards came racing towards me, ready to exchange their mount with mine. I considered not stopping. I was too close to waste any precious minutes, and time wasn't on my side. However, killing my horse—and maybe even myself in process once he fell—wouldn't help anyone. The fresher horses could cover the remaining distance much faster, anyway.

I slowed down, dismounted, and nearly tore my guard off his mount when he took too long getting off. I rode the beast hard, grateful for my decision at the heightened speed with which we reached the castle. Barely slowing my mount down, I jumped off mid-stride. The guards manning the entrance had already opened the door.

I ran in, screaming Astrid's name. I raced down the stairs to the dungeon, stunned that I didn't stumble and break my neck. In the distance ahead, I could hear multiple voices, among them Tormund and… Hilda?

"Your Highness, please. Do not enter the room, I beg you. King Erik will be here any minute. He will—"

"ASTRID!" I shouted, running to her.

She was standing right outside the door, her palms resting on each side of the doorframe. Astrid looked at me over her shoulder. Her golden skin appeared yellowish and sickly, her eyes glazed over. Her forehead was wrinkled with strain and covered with a thin layer of sweat.

"H–Hel–Help… M–Me…" Astrid begged.

I stopped just a couple of steps from her and spread my arms wide open, beckoning her. "Astrid… my love… come to me… Please, let go of the door and come to me."

"I–I've fai–failed…"

An evil laugh emanated from the room. My jaw dropped when I saw Hilda within, holding the medallion. In an instant, I realized what had happened. Astrid hadn't given in. She was still fighting. Hope surged within me.

"You haven't failed, my love. Hilda tricked you," I said. "*You* didn't open the door. You stayed true."

"Oh, do shut up, King Erik," Hilda said. Her voice dripped with contempt, but it wasn't just her voice: it was a mixture of Traxia's and hers. "You should have chosen *me*. Now you will lose everything, and I will rule the kingdom in your stead."

Ignoring Hilda, I focused on my wife, using my compulsion to lure her away. "Astrid, just give me your hand, love, and I will take care of everything. Come, my darling. Come to the one who loves you."

For a second, I thought Astrid wouldn't do it. Then she lifted a shaky hand off the doorframe. I only needed her to lift the second one before I could pull her away. The joint voices of Hilda and Traxia continued to try to entice Astrid, but she'd locked eyes with me. She placed her trembling hand in mine, her gaze fearful yet full of trust.

"Now, the other hand, my darling. Let go of the doorframe, my love," I coaxed gently.

As soon as she did, I pulled her into my embrace and dragged her away from the door. I wanted nothing more than to haul her back to our room, but only a few feet from the door, she began to spasm and gasp for breath.

The necklace... She cannot part from it until the seal is complete.

Too much distance would kill her.

"Tormund..." I called to my majordomo.

He held onto Astrid for me, after she reluctantly released me. I turned to face Hilda.

"You foolish woman. Your blind ambition is now your doom. So many good options would have been available to one of your beauty and rank. But that wasn't enough for you," I said in a harsh tone.

"Don't patronize me. We don't need that pathetic bride of yours. Using her would have hastened things, but with my aid, Traxia will prevail against you and make me Queen of the Rathlin Islands."

I marched to the Sealed Room, my emotions torn between pity and contempt. "Is that what she promised you, Hilda? She promised to give you my throne? And you believed her?"

"Her issue is with you."

"Is it? Yet, who keeps dying? Me or my brides? Have you forgotten how she brought our kingdom to its knees before I stopped her?" I asked, standing by the door frame.

Behind her, Traxia's image was slowly fading from the

psyche. I knew why she kept quiet, allowing Hilda and me to converse unimpeded: she needed the time.

"She will give me the same deal the original king had. She will rule the Kingdom of Llys, and I will rule Rathlin," Hilda said, lifting her chin defiantly.

"Wrong," I said, unsheathing my sword. Her eyes widened in fear. "Traxia never intended to give you anything. If you succeed, your body will sit on the throne, but it will be Traxia's mind occupying it. You were simply meant to be the vessel."

"But—"

"Look behind you," I interrupted mercilessly. "She's almost gone from the psyche, because she's taking possession of what you so eagerly offered—yourself."

Hilda looked back and began to tremble when the hollowed image of Traxia laughed at her. Hilda tried to get out of the room, but her feet wouldn't obey. I recognized that look all too well, having seen it too many times before, when Traxia took over control of my brides.

"Stop her! Please! I'm sorry!" Hilda pleaded. "I will accept whatever punishment—"

"Oh, I will stop her," I said, interrupting her, my tone frosty. "But you won't like how."

I looked over my shoulder to make sure Tormund kept Astrid's eyes averted. He knew what was coming next. I would spare her the horror. Bracing for Traxia's counterattack, I stepped into the room. My stomach churned from the malevolence of the dark magic within.

"What are you doing, Erik?" Hilda's voice shook with fear.

"What should have never needed to happen again," I said, raising my sword meaningfully.

"No!" Hilda shrieked, raising her hands protectively—not that it would have stopped me.

However, Hilda's defensive moves didn't concern me; Traxia's did. Right on cue, a wall of corals rose before me, shielding

Hilda from my blade. Hacking and slashing, I plowed my way through the endless waves of defenses. It had never been this hard before. Traxia's magic was stronger, faster. Then again, she'd never had a host who voluntarily let her in before. The others had tried to fight her but had been too weak.

Traxia's image in the psyche was flickering in and out of existence. I was running out of time. Once her image faded, she would have fully transferred her consciousness into Hilda's body and would be able to walk out of the Sealed Room. For the first time in fifteen years of face-offs with my Sea Witch sister, I felt true fear that I would fail to seal her back in. Hilda was emitting gurgling sounds in a last effort to cry out for help, but Traxia had taken away too much of her control. Hilda would soon be no more than a memory.

Panting, drenched in sweat, I tried to ignore the burn in my arms from the exertion. The attacks became more vicious. Some of the coral was now growing on the floor beneath my feet, knocking me off balance. Sharp, dagger-like shards shot out amidst the corals. A few of them only gave me slight nips and cuts, but one nearly buried itself in my gut. With a startled cry, I backed up, having never experienced this before. The coral built faster than I could destroy it, and the barbed shards slowed me down further.

Cold dread ran down my spine when the psyche flashed with a brilliant glow before its frame turned a dull, dead color. The corals receded revealing Traxia in the body of Hilda. Without the glow of the dead psyche, the room was pitched into darkness, aside from what light trickled in through the open door. With a wave of her hand, Traxia lit the sconces on the wall, revealing what the shadows had mercifully kept hidden thus far. I averted my eyes from the standing bodies of my previous wives lining the walls like statues; their beheaded corpses eternally preserved within a layer of coral. At their feet, their heads stared unseeing at the psyche.

"Hello, little brother," Traxia said, her voice chilling.

"I can't let you walk out of here, Traxia. I know how much damage and destruction you will visit upon my people."

The Sea Witch laughed. "*Your* people, brother? They're mine now. They always would have been had Father not despoiled me of my birthright. Time for you to go, usurper."

I raised my sword to strike at her, but with a flick of her wrist, she sent it flying right out of my hands. Before I knew what hit me, agony exploded in my back. I crashed into the wall with a loud thud. She had flung me across the room as if I weighed no more than a stone. Stunned, I tried to get back on my feet. Excruciating pain tore at me when sharp coral shards protruding from the ground pierced my back. Pinned down and weaponless, I watched in horror as Traxia slowly approached, strutting smugly until she stood towering over me.

"Time to die, little brother. Say hello to Father for me."

She raised her hand to cast the final spell that would end me when an angry shout resonated behind her. Startled, we both turned to see Astrid descending upon Traxia with my sword in her upraised hands. Eyes wide with fear, Traxia opened her mouth, probably to order Astrid to stand down with her siren voice. But my wife sliced Traxia's head neatly off her shoulders before she could utter a word.

"Stay away from my husband, you demon!" Astrid yelled at the shuddering corpse at my feet.

Tossing the sword to the ground, Astrid raced to my side, her face strained with worry. The coral shards impaling me receded, tearing a pained shout out of me. It was drowned by the shrill shrieks of Traxia as her essence was pulled back into the psyche. The incredibly loud sound forced Astrid and I to cover our ears. When the scream finally stopped, wincing with pain, I forced myself up with Astrid's aid.

I snatched the necklace out of Hilda's limp hand. Seconds later, coral tendrils pulled her corpse and head to a vacant spot on the wall, next to Ariana's remains, to be preserved as well. I turned Astrid towards me, so she wouldn't continue staring at the macabre spectacle, and then placed the necklace around her neck. Immediately, she seemed to breathe better, and her sigh of relief indicated whatever pain she had been in had faded.

Fighting to stay steady despite the blood dripping out of me, I led Astrid out of the room. "Come on, my darling. We need to reseal the door."

Ignoring Traxia's venomous shouts from within her crystal prison, we stepped out of this den of despair. My eyes full of awe, I watched the most amazing woman, the love of my life, shut the door and re-activate the seals with unshakeable resolve.

"You are wounded," Astrid said, wrapping an arm around my waist to support me.

"Astrid... You just saved both of our lives and that of every living soul in both realms, and you're worried about my wounds?"

She stared at me in concern. "You're hurt, Erik. I saw you fly across the room and crash against the wall. There's..."

"I'm fine, my darling," I said, leaning in to kiss her.

She leaned back out of reach and put her palm on my chest, stopping me. "You're bleeding." Turning to Tormund, who stared at us with his mouth gaping, Astrid gestured for him to come forward. "Master Tormund, help me get him back to our room and send for the physician."

"Y–Yes, your Highness," Tormund said, rushing to our side. He stole awed glances at Astrid the whole way up to our room. I couldn't blame him.

Although bruised and bleeding, I climbed my way out of the dungeon the happiest of men.

EPILOGUE
ASTRID

Today was the last day of my trial. Three days had gone by since the insane confrontation with Traxia. Three days during which Erik made a swift recovery from his injuries, thanks to his Llysian blood. The best part of it all was that Traxia's plan had backfired spectacularly.

Something snapped inside of me when I saw the man I loved about to be murdered. Filled with blind rage, the only thing driving me had been the need to destroy the threat. As if in a dream, I had picked up Erik's sword and made quick work of the abomination that had made his life a living hell for a decade and a half.

But severing her head from her body did more than end her rebirth through Hilda as a vessel. Somehow, it also terminated the link she had established between us. It was as if at that specific moment, I had so violently rejected her and everything she stood for that I had erected a wall between us—a wall she could no longer break through. While I could still hear Traxia's endless screams for me to come to her, her words no longer lured or enticed. Her powers of compulsion over me belonged to the past.

Erik kept saying I had saved us all, but we had saved each other. Even though I had given the final blow, without his steadfast help through the painful last few months, Tormund's intervention while Erik raced back from the village, and my husband's attack on the possessed Hilda, there was no question I would have fallen. However, today, the ordeal would end forever.

As Erik and I walked towards the entrance of the dungeon, the servants lined the hallway, bowing to us as we passed. For the first time, all of them made eye contact with me. My throat tightened at the blatant joy and gratitude in their eyes. As we approached, a pair of guards opened the door to the dungeon.

Erik and I climbed down, for what I hoped would be the last time, with Tormund shadowing us. The fully charged medallion hanging from my neck glowed brightly like the sun at its zenith. The last dull seal beckoned me. Stepping up to the Sealed Door, I placed the medallion in its socket. Traxia's screams became one long banshee shriek, but it held no sway over me, other than its painful loudness.

"Welcome to your eternal hell, demon," I whispered, then resolutely turned the medallion to the left.

As its gem drained of energy, it felt as if my soul was being torn out of my body. The pain was excruciating, but I embraced it. This sacrifice would ensure my 'happily ever after.' The energy flowed through the carved vines on the door up to the final seal on the wall, just beyond the doorframe. Once the seal was activated, the entire wall pulsed with a blinding light.

My scream of pain mixed with Traxia's desperate shouts. As the glow receded, the seam of the doorframe vanished. The only indications a door ever stood there were the medallion socket and glowing tendrils stemming from it to the pulsating seals. It reminded me of a magical rising sun on the horizon.

Traxia's voice suddenly fell silent, and the agony of the transfer faded. I collapsed, but Erik's muscular arms caught me.

He crushed my lips with a passionate kiss and held me in a bruising embrace. Feeling dazed and groggy, I weakly embraced him, laughing and crying.

"It's over, my darling. You've done it! We're free at last. My beloved wife…"

"I told you I would be the last one…" I slurred.

He chuckled softly, his forehead resting against mine. "Yes, you did."

Erik picked me up and carried me to our room under the teary cheers and applause of the guards and servants. I didn't see them though: my eyes were only for my beloved husband. He laid me down on our bed and removed the necklace from my neck.

I stared at him wide-eyed. "What…?"

"You don't need this anymore, my darling. I'll put this away where no greedy hands can ever access it again. As for you, my love," he said, kissing the tip of my nose, "I will put a different piece of jewelry on you tomorrow, when your father gives you away at the altar."

"My father? Wait… what?"

"Tomorrow, we marry. The entire realm will bear witness as I take my true wife. Thank you, Astrid, for remaining strong. I love you so much. The thought of losing you…"

"You will never lose me, Erik. Not today, not tomorrow, not ever. I love you now and always."

ERIK

Following Traxia's demise, as much as I reveled in my newfound freedom, I struggled with the lingering trauma of the past fifteen years. The first few weeks, I would wake up with a start and pinch myself to make sure this was indeed reality, that our victory hadn't been an illusion.

Although we gradually reinstated the number of live-in servants and guards in the castle, their mere presence had me constantly on the verge of paranoia. Hearing their hushed voices inside the castle walls at night nearly gave me heart attacks until my mind caught up with the fact that it wasn't Traxia whispering in my head.

In direct contrast, Astrid was thriving. In truth, a radical change had occurred from the moment she had beheaded Hilda possessed by Traxia. My wife had become bolder, more assertive, stronger, and fearless. There was an aura of power about her that commanded respect while also being incredibly enticing.

The people adored her.

It went well beyond the fact that she had ended the curse and brought back peace and prosperity to the realm. She exuded an incredible aura of benevolence. It wrapped around you like a mother's love, and everyone wanted to bask in it. During our first diplomatic travels, simply having her by my side made negotiations go so much smoother. All it took was a smile from her, and people melted.

Something had definitely happened that day. Thankfully, it only seemed to have positive effects on my beloved.

Two months after the curse ended, Astrid announced that she was pregnant with our first child. Considering the multiple miscarriages my mother had suffered because of the dark magic from the psyche, I had wanted to keep it quiet until Astrid's bump clearly started showing. However, I kept those misgivings to myself. I didn't want to dampen my wife's happiness, and I feared voicing my concerns would draw bad luck upon our child.

Anyway, Inga had confirmed the dark magic from the mirror had been completely sealed off in the room. Traxia's bond with the kraken had also been severed, the formidable creature now only responding to my will or to those I authorized.

For all my excessive worry, the pregnancy went off without a hitch. And on the first day of December, exactly nine months after the curse ended, Astrid gave birth to our daughter. We named her Alinor after my grandmother. She was stunning, born under a clear blue sky and with unusually warm weather for the season.

Sitting at the edge of the bed, one arm wrapped around Astrid's shoulders, I gazed with awe at our child cradled in her mother's arms.

"She has your angelic face and your beautiful golden blond hair," I said tenderly, my voice choked with emotion.

"But with your amazing silver eyes and your gills," Astrid whispered before cooing at our daughter, her slender fingers tracing the barely visible lines on our child's neck.

I smiled, silencing the unease wanting to set root in the pit of my stomach. Traxia had also been blonde with silver eyes. Obviously, it was merely a coincidence. After all, my grandfather and wife were blonde. It made sense for our daughter to inherit those traits.

"The perfect mix of the two of us," I said affectionately.

And perfect, she was.

Everyone would fawn over her, even the servants found every possible excuse to be near her. They didn't realize part of it was due to her siren songs. As with every Llysian child, Alinor instinctively vocalized, usually when feeling strong emotions from joy to sadness, or discomforts from hunger to needing her diaper changed. But as a happy child, she usually drew people to her out of joy.

It was still night outside, in the wee hours of the morning of the first anniversary of Traxia's defeat, when I felt a shift in the air. First, my skin tingled with what I recognized as the kraken's power surging through me. Then I heard my daughter's call.

Astrid stirred against me, her eyes snapping open. She didn't seem dazed or confused, as one normally would after awakening.

She immediately locked gazes with me. "Alinor needs us," she said, matter-of-factly.

"You hear her?" I asked, slightly taken aback.

Astrid nodded. "I *always* hear her," she replied, as if it was self-evident.

We got out of bed and slipped on our sleeping tunics before entering our daughter's bedroom, adjacent to ours. Wide awake, she leveled her silver eyes on us, her heart-shaped mouth stretched in a toothless grin as she beamed at us.

Through the window facing the ocean in the distance, thunderclouds were gathering over the water. Yet, they held no menace, only promises. Simultaneously, hundreds of voices rose in the distance in a haunting melody. No one but those it was intended for would hear it.

"Your people... They're calling," Astrid said, sounding intrigued, not afraid.

"Yes," I replied.

"They want to meet her," she added, with almost prophetic accuracy.

"Yes," I said again, studying her features to see her reaction.

"Then let's go meet them," she said with a smile.

I smiled back, picked up our daughter and led the way to the secret passage in my study. Barefoot like me, Astrid didn't seem to mind the cool stones beneath our feet as we walked down the tunnel to the secret cove. With each step the melody grew stronger. However, this time we could hear it both in our minds and in our ears. Alinor cooed and giggled, her excitement intensifying the closer we got to our destination.

"By the Gods!" Astrid whispered when we finally exited the passage.

Hundreds of Llysians stood on the incline where the patches of grass had given way to the sand licked by the tidal waves. Many more stood in the water or swam in it. Queen Eira and Sea Witch Inga stood straight ahead of us on the beach. And in the water, the massive silhouette of the kraken rose behind them, its yellow eyes glowing like two giant beacons in the night.

Astrid slipped a hand in mine. Their mesmerizing chant faded as we closed the distance with my aunt.

"Hello Erik, and you, Astrid," my aunt said in a warm tone before turning her gaze to our daughter still cradled in my arms.

While they had not attended our wedding, Aunt Eira, Inga, and a few other Llysians had come to meet Astrid on a few occasions by entering the castle through the secret passage.

"It is good to see you again, Eira," Astrid replied in a similar tone, while I smiled at my aunt.

"And there she is, the little wonder that has had us all enthralled," Eira continued.

"Enthralled?" I repeated, confused.

"Your little princess has been singing to the kraken since her birth. But over the past few weeks, she has been singing to us," Inga explained.

I stiffened, worry crashing over me.

"It is a *good* song, Erik," Eira interjected rapidly, no doubt in response to my expression. "A *very good* song."

Astrid and I exchanged a confused glance before casting an inquisitive look at my aunt.

"It is a Queen's song, a rallying song. Only a true Llysian Queen can unite us in perfect harmony. Alinor isn't your heir. She is *ours*," Eira continued.

"The Kraken has bonded with her," Inga added. "She is not just our future queen, but also one of the most powerful Sea Witches of all times. When I met Astrid, I had wondered whose powers I felt—hers or the child she was bearing. Now, I know it was both."

"Both?" Astrid asked, echoing my thoughts, although I suspected what would follow.

"The day you slew Traxia's vessel, you absorbed her magic and passed it down to your child. And I suspect you will do the same for each of your offspring," Inga explained. "As you are not Llysian, you will not be able to harness its power the way one of us would."

"But she passively exerts it," I said, understanding dawning on me.

Inga nodded. "But your daughter will rule the seas and the elements. Her heart is pure. So raise her well. And when the son you currently bear is born, nurture the love and harmony between them. Together, they will reign over this world."

My jaw dropped, and Astrid pressed a palm to her still flat stomach.

"A son? I'm carrying a son?" she whispered, joy and shock lighting up her beautiful eyes.

"Yes, my dear. You're carrying your kingdom's heir," Eira said affectionately. "Through your children, our worlds will finally come together. No more secrets."

My heart filling with love and happiness, I turned to my wife, and exchanged a kiss full of devotion. We broke the kiss, eyes locked with each other for a few seconds. Alinor cooed, her tiny hand stretching to caress Astrid's cheek and then mine.

"But for this future to occur, Erik, you must willingly yield the reins to your daughter," Inga interjected, drawing our attention back to the people surrounding us. "The kraken will still follow your biddings, but once little Alinor comes of age, he will defer to her."

"I consent," I replied without hesitation. "I do not crave this type of power."

Eira's face melted with affection as she smiled approvingly. "Then present your daughter to her bond and protector."

With my arms around Astrid's waist, I walked to the edge of the water. Alinor wiggled and giggled, her small hands reaching for the creature that would otherwise have most people running for the hills.

The kraken came closer, his giant tentacles spreading in our direction. I almost expected Astrid to recoil or attempt to back away. But she stood still, a trusting expression on her features as the tip of dark gray tentacle caressed Alinor's arm before wrapping around her. I released our daughter, who continued to giggle and beam at the creature.

To my surprise, the kraken extended a second tentacle, this time, gently brushing it over Astrid's stomach, acknowledging our unborn son. My wife further pressed herself against me, my arm around her tightened its hold.

As the voices of my Llysian family rose again, we watched in awe as lightning danced behind the clouds overhead, and our little princess hugged the tentacle of the most fearsome creature in the seven seas.

There would be no more temptations, no more threats to our realm.

We had won.

THE END

ERIK

ALSO BY REGINE ABEL

THE VEREDIAN CHRONICLES
Escaping Fate
Blind Fate
Raising Amalia
Twist of Fate
Hands of Fate
Defying Fate

BRAXIANS
Anton's Grace
Ravik's Mercy
Krygor's Hope

XIAN WARRIORS
Doom
Legion
Raven
Bane
Chaos
Varnog
Reaper
Wrath
Xenon
Nevrik

PRIME MATING AGENCY
I Married A Lizardman
I Married A Naga
I Married A Birdman
I Married A Minotaur
I Married A Merman

I Married A Dragon
I Married A Beast
I Married A Dryad

THE MIST
The Mistwalker
The Nightmare

DARK TALES
Bluebeard's Curse
The Hunchback

BLOOD MAIDENS OF KARTHIA
Claiming Thalia

VALOS OF SONHADRA
Unfrozen
Iced

EMPATHS OF LYRIA
An Alien For Christmas

THE SHADOW REALMS
Dark Swan

OTHER
True As Steel
Alien Awakening
Heart of Stone

ABOUT REGINE

USA Today bestselling author Regine Abel is a fantasy, para-normal and sci-fi junky. Anything with a bit of magic, a touch of the unusual, and a lot of romance will have her jumping for joy. She loves creating hot alien warriors and no-nonsense, kick-ass heroines that evolve in fantastic new worlds while embarking on action-packed adventures filled with mystery and the twists you never saw coming.

Before devoting herself as a full-time writer, Regine had surren-dered to her other passions: music and video games! After a decade working as a Sound Engineer in movie dubbing and live concerts, Regine became a professional Game Designer and Creative Director, a career that has led her from her home in Canada to the US and various countries in Europe and Asia.

Facebook
  https://www.facebook.com/regine.abel.author/

Website
  https://regineabel.com

Regine's Rebels Reader Group
https://www.facebook.com/groups/ReginesRebels/

Newsletter
http://smarturl.it/RA_Newsletter

Goodreads
http://smarturl.it/RA_Goodreads

Bookbub
https://www.bookbub.com/profile/regine-abel

Amazon
http://smarturl.it/AuthorAMS

Made in the USA
Middletown, DE
02 March 2025

71987474R00115